Journey's End

The Legacy Saga

J. Adams

J. Adams

Copyright © 2015 J. Adams
ISBN-13: 978-0692536926
ISBN-10: 0692536922
Library of Congress Control Number: 2015915399
Jewel of the West Publishing
All Rights Reserved

Jewel of the West™
PUBLISHING

To all my Legacy fans,

Thanks for hanging in there to the very end!

I appreciate ya!

J. Adams

IV

Prologue

Treviso, Italy

"*It* is all right, *amore*. Shhh, it will be okay."

Oh, Heavenly Father, this hurts so much.

I shudder as a torrent of tears spill from my sightless eyes, soaking the front of my husband's t-shirt. We lay in bed and he rocks me slowly, emotion cracking his voice as he croons words of comfort.

I have lost another baby and my heart is shattering. This loss is even more painful than the last time. The first was last year–a honeymoon baby–and I loved it from the moment I read the positive test result.

A month later, I was out pruning the rose bushes when the cramping started. That evening my pregnancy ended, and we were devastated.

After I healed, we began to try again and two months ago, we were finally successful. Sadly, yesterday the familiar cramps started again. And this morning, to my sorrow, I lost the baby. This time the pain is more than I can bear. I have stayed in bed all morning and Adagio has not left my side.

Keeping my head pressed against his chest, I silently ask the same question over and over.

Why? Why can't I have a baby? Why can't I give my husband a child?

You know why, comes the familiar reply in my deceased father's voice. **Because you're worthless. If we hadn't adopted you, you would probably be living out on the streets somewhere following in the footsteps of your drug addict mother. After all, that's why you were born blind.**

I'm not worthless!

Yes, you're a broken soul and not good for much of anything.

No! My mind slams shut the mental gate that has

always protected my heart from Father's hateful and vile words. He had been an evil man, and when he died, I had been more relieved than anything. When he was alive, he did his best to make me feel worthless, and soon he began to treat Mother the same way. Deep inside, I know God loves and values me more than that.

But why does this keep happening?

As if he can read my thoughts–and I really believe he can at times–Adagio whispers against my brow, "You mean everything to me, Evangeline. Nothing is more important to me, and I know that when the time is right, we will be blessed with a child. When that time does come, nothing will stop it. As long as we have faith, any and everything is possible."

Smiling against his cheek, I whisper, "I know." Drawing back a little, I tearfully raise my eyes to his face, just making out his shadowed outline. I can feel the warmth of his gaze. "Thank you for reminding me. And for loving me."

He touches his lips to mine and I feel him smile. "Always."

Relaxing on a blanket out on the back lawn,

Adagio lay with his head in my lap. With my eyes closed, I tip my head back, enjoying the sun's warmth, and slowly run my fingers through his hair, gently massaging his scalp. A gentle breeze flows over us, bringing with it the scent of the river. I know my surroundings. Though I have never seen them I know, because Adagio has painted the picture for me and I see it all through his eyes. I see the rolling green lawn, the red and yellow buds on the rose bushes, the birds flying overhead in the brilliant blue sky. With my husband's descriptive words, I have seen more during our marriage than I ever did before, and I am grateful for these tender mercies.

Because Adagio's parents are away on an extended vacation, we have the villa to ourselves. I wish I had more energy to take advantage of this time and do something fun for Adagio. As it is, I feel completely useless.

For a moment, a small degree of pity briefly enters my heart, and for an instant, I wonder if Adagio ever has second thoughts about marrying me. As soon as the thought enters my mind, guilt fills me and beg God for forgiveness.

Adagio

Adagio opens his eyes and looks up at his wife's face, immediately reading her thoughts in her expression. She may not be able to see, but her beautiful, light brown eyes say more than she knows. His heart grieves for her and their loss. But more than that, Adagio aches inside because he knows Evangeline has lost sight of her true worth. Closing his eyes again, he prays for a moment, and inspiration quickly comes, something that has been happening to him a lot more lately.

He sits up and cups her cheek. "*Cuoricina mia,* sweetheart, sit here for a bit and I will be right back, all right?"

"Okay."

Adagio quickly runs up to their bedroom. It had been his grandparents' room before they died. Adagio's father had insisted that Adagio and Evangeline move into the room when they were married. On the day that he'd cleaned out the closet to fill it with their own things, he'd found an envelope beneath a box that contained a few sentimental trinkets belonging to his grandparents. The box and the envelope were addressed to him. Attached to the envelope was a note written in his grandmother's hand that said, *Young Adagio, the letter inside is for your wife.*

Adagio had completely forgotten about the letter until now. Maybe there was a reason. After all, God does know what His children need when they need it.

Adagio removes the envelope addressed to his wife and takes it out to her.

I hear Adagio's approaching footsteps and see his shadow coming closer. He sits next to me and places an envelope in my hands.

"What is it?" I ask.

"This is a letter to you from my grandmother. There was a note attached that said it was for my wife. I found it last year when we moved into the room, but I had actually forgotten about it until now."

I am so surprised, I don't know what to say. I already look up to Adagio's grandparents a great deal and have gotten to know them through their journals. I wish I could have really known them. To be holding a letter from his grandmother leaves me in awe. I hold it out to Adagio. "Will you read it?"

"I would be happy to." He opens the envelope and begins.

Dear Mrs. St. John,

First, let me say how happy I am that you and Adagio found each other. You must be an amazing woman to have won my grandson's heart. I always knew God had someone truly special picked out for him, and Adagio can tell you that his **nonna** *is never wrong.*

I chuckle. "Was she ever wrong?"

Adagio laughs. "Never." He continues reading.

My grandson has probably shared a little about us with you, maybe even shared our journals. I hope he has since we can't be there. Even though we aren't there to know you, you can get to know us through our words. Young Adagio always said he wanted to find a woman just like his **nonna**. *I assured him that he would find someone much better, and though I am not there, I know he has, because that was always my prayer for him–that he would marry his other half, a woman with integrity and inner-strength. Someone possessing qualities that would make him a better man* *simply by being with her. I know that someone is you.*

You are going to have both good and bad times. You will have trials and triumphs, and you will live through experiences that will test your faith to the point that you'll wonder how you will make it through. But all of these things are learning experiences and will only make you stronger than you already are. Always remember to lean on God and He will see you through everything you will face in this life. The Savior knows your heart. He knows your joys and your sorrows because He has felt them all, and He will always be there. Adagio was taught this as a young boy and he has never strayed from it.

Your husband is a good man. He is just like his grandfather. He loves with his whole heart and soul, and I know he loves you with all that he is. Never doubt that love. And never doubt your worth. My grandson will treat you like the queen that you are and you will both be very blessed. I promise you this.

I love you more than I can say. Thank you for making my grandson so happy. Now that you have each other-and God-you have everything. And that is *everything.*

Nonna

I smile as Adagio gently wipes the tears streaking my face. He draws me into his arms and I bury my face against his shoulder.

"I can't believe it!" I whisper. "How did she know? How did she know I would need her words?"

"My grandmother was an inspired woman. My grandfather always said she had a gift."

"I'm grateful she was so in tune with the Lord."

"So am I."

Sighing, I smile, raising my face toward the heavens. I will be okay now. No matter what happens in the future–whether I have a baby or we have to adopt, I will be okay. With Adagio by my side, I will make it through. Lifting a hand to my husband's face, I caress the beloved handsome Italian features I have never seen.

"*Ti amo*, Adagio."

Lowering his lips to mine, he kisses me languorously. "*Ti amo, angelo.*"

The following summer, Evangeline gives birth to Adagio Phillip St. John IV. With a midwife standing by to assist, Adagio delivers the baby and it is one of the most spiritual experiences they have ever had. The little boy is beautiful and perfect, and the proud parents feel beyond blessed.

Evangeline has no idea, however, how much the trials and triumphs in her life have been preparing her for the coming times. The world is ever-changing, the hope of human hearts fading more by the day.

Evangeline's place in the world is more important than she knows.

And it shall come to pass in the last days, saith God, I will pour out my Spirit upon all flesh: and your sons and your daughters shall prophesy, and your young men shall see visions, and your old men shall dream dreams:

Acts 2:17

J. Adams

Chapter 1

When God blessed me with Evangeline, he blessed me with a guiding star.

Adagio St. John's Journal

Five Years Later

Treviso, Italy

"I can see you! You are both so beautiful!"

Adagio's grandmother presses a hand to my cheek. "Thank you, Evangeline." She smiles at her husband, the man Adagio was named after.

"Does Adagio really look like you?" I ask him.

"Exactly like me," he answers with a smile, his

emerald eyes twinkling merrily. He squeezes my hand. "Evangeline, it is time for you and young Adagio to leave."

"Leave? Why must we leave?"

"Because your life is not here."

"But . . . where will we go?"

Cisely smiles. "Back to where it began. It is God's will."

Back to where it began. To where our family began. *Conviction fills my heart.* "We will go wherever Heavenly Father wants us to go."

Adagio nods. "He knows this, which is why He brought you and our grandson together." His expression is solemn. "Your little family has faithfully lived the gospel of Jesus Christ. You were baptized into His church and took upon you His name. Now your family is an eternal one. You have shared your testimony of the gospel by word and example, and as a result, it is now the binding tie for our entire family. Your work here is done. The rest of the family will continue on from here. Now you must go."

"We love you," Cisely says, her silky voice warm. "Always remember that." *A slight furrow appears between her brows.* "Tribulation is coming, but you will not go through it alone. You will never be alone."

They each kiss my brow, then they take each other's hand and walk down the veranda steps and across the lawn before fading away.

Another voice draws my attention and I turn.

"I know you," I whisper as He draws closer.

He smiles, holding a large hand out to me and I place mine in it. There is a deep mark in His palm and I am briefly saddened by it. Then He says my name and His voice pierces my heart, and I suddenly surrounded in such warmth, it is like my spirit is on fire, yet there is a peace I have never known. I look into his eyes. I have never truly seen the color blue, but the shade of his eyes is vivid–like sapphires is the description that clearly comes to mind.

"Evangeline," He repeats, opening His arms and I move into His embrace, wrapping my own arms around Him, and I weep tears of joy as His love flows over me, through me.

"Stay with me," I softly plead.

Pressing a kiss to my brow, He whispers, "I am with you always."

My eyes suddenly open and I sit up, drying the tears I'd shed in my sleep. The bedroom is still dim, but I can make out the soft light coming through the window, which tells me it is still early. Adagio's side of the bed is empty. The coolness of his pillows means he has been up for a while. I reach over and touch the braille clock on my nightstand. It is only 5:30, but I get up. I need to find him and share the incredible experience I was just given. Apart from marrying him and having our son, this is the most amazing thing that has ever happened to me.

The tile floor is cool beneath my bare feet as I quietly search for him. Dagio is still sleeping, and Phillip and Mali, Adagio's parents, are not up yet.

"Adagio," I softly call, wandering from the family room to the kitchen, but he does not answer. I make my way back through the family room to the veranda doors. Finding one of them slightly open, I slip outside.

"I'm here," comes his beloved voice. Taking my hand, he guides me to our usual spot on the veranda. He sits in one of the wicker chairs and pulls me onto his lap. His arms enfold me and I rest my brow against his as we silently take in the peaceful morning sounds.

I take a moment to ponder the dream. It was a beautiful and sacred experience. I only hope Adagio will give some thought and consideration to what I will share with him. Deep down, I know he will.

As I open my mouth to begin, he says, "I had an experience, *amore*."

My heart skipping a beat, I bury my fingers in his hair. "Tell me."

"I don't know if you will believe me."

Pressing my lips against his ear, I whisper, "Tell me."

"My grandparents came to me."

I caress his face, silently urging him to continue.

"I could not sleep. I didn't know why. I came out here to sit for a moment . . . and suddenly they were here. They were young again–our age, I am guessing, maybe closer to yours. I was so happy to see them, I cried."

I can hear the tears in his voice, feel fresh ones rolling down his face and I hold him closer.

"They said it was time for us to leave, to go back where we began, to where our family began. They said our work here is done and it is Heavenly Father's will that we leave. *Nonna* said tribulation is coming, but we won't have to face it alone. Oh, Evangeline, it was incredible!"

I cover my mouth as a river of tears stream down my face.

"What is it?" he asks, cupping my cheek.

Shaking my head, I bury my face against his neck, unable to speak. For a few moments, I just let him hold me, absorbing the enormity of it all. Finally, I share my dream with him, imagining the awe that I am sure is filling his expression.

"Adagio, to be able to see them . . . to see *you* when I looked at your grandfather . . ." I pause, touching his face, caressing the soft stubble on his cheek. "There are no words."

He releases a deep breath. "I can't believe it!" he breathes. "It is . . . There really are no words."

"There is more," I say, my voice growing softer, a feeling of deep reverence filling me. Adagio silently waits for me to go on. "When your grandparents left, someone called my name–a man. I turned, and I knew who he was the moment I saw him." Squeezing his hand, my voice is barely a whisper. "I saw the nail print in His hand when He reached out to me. I felt it when I placed my hand in His."

"You saw the Savior?" Adagio's voice is a whisper, his fingers tightening around mine.

"I felt His embrace–was surrounded by the comforting warmth of His love. I asked Him to stay with me and . . . He said He would be with me always."

Holding me close, I feel a quiet sob roll through him. "Oh, angel!"

We cling to each other with humble gratitude in our hearts for the miraculous gift we have been given, this mutual event strengthening our individual testimony of this truly being the final days before the Savior's return.

J. Adams

Chapter 2

The Lord's sifting process began ages ago and the harvesting is now in progress.

Sadly, as prophesied, the number of tares far outweighs the volume of wheat.

Adagio St. John's Journal

Salt Lake City, Utah
Two months later

$\mathcal{T}$he city has changed a great deal since we were here three years ago to visit my mother. It seems a little . . . I guess, colder. The people seem colder, not all but some. A city that was once filled with genuinely good people who strived to be Christ-like and decent human beings has slowly been changed to one I would most likely not recognize even if I could see. Of course, it is the same throughout the country, and the world. But for me, and Adagio as well, it is more noticeable here.

However, I remind myself daily that there is still a lot of good. That good can be found in the hearts of the faithful, those who have watched for the signs and can see past the mounting tribulation and recognize God's hand in all things.

I ponder on these things as Adagio and I water the vegetable garden and flower patches. Dagio splashes in the large shallow kiddie pool we purchased to help him stay cool during the sweltering July days. We placed it near the patio where we are able to keep tabs on him until Mom comes. She will be here soon to take him out for ice-cream and a movie. There is nothing she enjoys more than spoiling her grandson.

Despite the heartache Mom has been through, she is doing very well. After Father died over seven years ago, I wondered if she would ever heal or truly be okay. Her marriage to him was an emotional trial, as well as a refiner's fire, and toward the end she underwent an inner change. Two years ago, she embraced the Lord's gospel and became a new person. Sometimes it is hard to believe the warm compassionate woman I know now is the same cold and unfeeling person who raised me. Once Father was gone, it was easier for God to work in her heart. How grateful I am for the privilege of really getting to know my mother, the real person, the person she was always meant to be.

Mom soon arrives and Dagio dries off and changes, excited to spend time with his 'Grandma Kat.' He still misses his grandparents in Italy, but he has enjoyed getting to know my mother. Her presence has helped to smooth the transition.

"We'll be back by four," Mom tells us.

"That sounds good," I say, kissing Dagio's cheek.

"You and Adagio should do something fun with the time."

"We will," Adagio says. "I am taking your beautiful daughter out to lunch."

She makes a soft noise of approval. "Good man."

"He is," I agree and Adagio kisses my cheek. "He's the best."

After they leave, we change and Adagio treats me to lunch at the City Creek mall. It is Saturday and the food court is humming with the voices of teens out of school for the summer.

Sitting at a table by the windows near the exit, for the first time in a long time, I find myself straining to focus on the shadows moving to and fro. This startles me because I have not felt that need since my first date with Adagio years ago. I smile slightly, remembering how I was quickly falling in love and had wished so badly that I could see him. Thinking on this current urge to focus in spite of my blindness, I realize it is most likely because of the dream. During those precious moments, I was given a glimpse of the world. For the first time, I could clearly see color, and people. When I dreamed before, there were never pictures. Even if there had been, I wouldn't have known what I was seeing anyway. My dreams had been made up of muted colors, shadows, and music. Always music. Now, interspersed with the muted shades are snapshots of memories, a second here, a second there, but never enough to make up the entire scene.

Through my husband's grandfather, I was able to see the handsome man I married. I saw his green eyes, his thick, black hair, his full lips, and the light stubble covering his chiseled jaw. With his height and muscular build, I know now without a doubt that I am an envied woman.

But as amazing as it was to see Adagio's grandparents, the most glorious part of the dream – and the most memorable – was seeing my Savior, feeling his loving embrace, and absorbing His glorious spirit, as well as His promise that He would never leave me alone.

"You're remembering, aren't you?" Adagio softly asks. He is always able to read me so easily.

"I am." I release a soft sigh. "It's still so amazing to me and . . ."

"And?"

"And I . . ." I don't know how to say it without sounding ungrateful, like speaking the words out loud might offend God. *Like he doesn't know my thoughts anyway.*

"What is it?"

His soft imploring draws my emotions closer to the surface. I speak as softly as I can, not wanting anyone to overhear. "I'm grateful for such a wonderful experience, but . . . I wish . . . That small glimpse made me want more. It wasn't enough and it should have been. I should be happy, Adagio. I shouldn't want more, but I do." I blink the tears away and Adagio's hand tightens on mine. "To see you, to see Dagio . . ." I take a deep breath, attempting to purge myself of the selfish thoughts and manage to draw forth a smile. "I'm okay."

When Adagio finally speaks, emotion is thick in his voice. "One day, *cuoricino mia*. One day you will see me, and you will see our son. Until then, this is what we have." He presses one of my hands against his face. "Whenever you need to see me, just touch me. This is *your* face. It belongs to you." His voice has grown softer and raspier, the deep tone causing my breaths to come faster.

"Adagio . . ."

My single breathing of his name says everything.

"Let's go home, angel."

Adagio

When they arrive home, Adagio leads his wife up to their room. It is the same room his grandparents shared when they were alive and stayed there, and for that reason, Adagio and Evangeline had chosen it for their own.

Closing the door, Adagio takes his wife's hands and gently presses her fingers over his closed eyes.

"See me, Evangeline," he breathes. "I'm yours. Look at me. These are your eyes." He moves her hands over his face, shuddering as her hitched breathing tingles his skin. Moving her fingers to his mouth, he whispers against them, "These are your lips." He releases her long enough to take off his shirt. Drawing her hands down his muscular chest, he holds them against his pounding heart. "Feel how my heart beats for you."

Then he presses his mouth to hers, attempting to convey his never-ending longing for her. "You do see me, *amore*," he rasps against the soft skin of her cheek. "Better than anyone."

"I see you, *amore mio*," she murmurs huskily,

pressing herself against him, the two melting into one another.

And for the next while, passion roams freely as emotion and need merge uninhibited and unrestrained.

Chapter 3

For every ten hearts that close, God's opens another. For every ten souls who refuse to see, one soul allows their vision to be clarified.

Adagio St. John's Journal

Two Days Later
Atlanta, Georgia

Bishop Greg Larsen has only one major regret in his life, and he hopes and prays that he will soon be able to make amends for that mistake.

Through the years, Greg's moments of reflection have grown more frequent, his thoughts much deeper.

His character has developed into one possessing caring and empathy, his greatest desire being, to be at one with his Savior and his Heavenly Father. Once upon a time, this was not the case.

Sitting behind the desk in his church office on this late Sunday evening, Greg ponders his life, and the events and choices that have brought him to this point.

Raised in a life of poverty by a wonderful woman who did the best she could to care for him, Greg had loved his mother very much. However, though he was grateful for her efforts, he harbored anger and resentment toward the father he'd never known. The man had made promises to his mother, then he'd left her pregnant and alone.

Greg's grandparents were affluent, having inherited millions in old money, and lived in a very prominent neighborhood. Choosing to keep up appearances rather than help their pregnant daughter, they kicked her out, completely disowning her. Greg grew up watching his mother work hard to provide a living for him. Some would say she worked herself to death. She finally died of a heart attack. Greg was only sixteen.

Somehow Greg fell through the proverbial cracks of society and was left on his own. Sleeping on park benches and behind abandoned buildings, he survived by washing dishes in a Chinese restaurant five nights a week. He continued to attend school and graduated. Then he went to trade school for a year, became an auto mechanic and moved in with a friend. After working at an auto repair shop for four years, he acquired a bank loan and bought the business from the ailing owner. He slowly turned the empty space above the shop into an apartment and moved in.

Greg was twenty-four when he met Althea Hines. He was sitting in a bar sipping a beer when she approached him. With her dark skin, long curvy body and braided hair, she was exotic and a temptation he didn't fight. He was lonely and she offered warm comfort for the night, and he took it.

But just one night with Althea had not been enough, so he offered something she did not really want: permanence. She agreed to stay, but deep down he knew she wasn't really his. Nevertheless, he pretended.

Althea had always been a drinker, but her drug

use was a new discovery, one that he quickly grew tired of.

The day she told him she was pregnant was the day she left, and he never went after her.

Seven months later he was called and told Althea passed away from an overdose, but not before giving birth to a tiny little girl. Giving up all claim to the child, Greg moved on and tried to forget. The child was soon adopted.

But even after thirty-two years, Greg has not forgotten. The knowledge that he has a daughter somewhere in the world, a precious child he'd given up the opportunity to know and love, hurts deeply.

And he truly does love her. No, he doesn't know her. He does not know what she looks like, how she grew up, if she has a family, or even if she still lives. But she fills his thoughts every day.

No, he does not know her.

But he loves her more than he'd thought possible.

Six years ago, Page Placido, a petite, dark-haired Brazilian beauty with lovely brown eyes and an amazing smile, brought her car to Greg's shop for repairs and the two were instantly taken with each other. In a matter of weeks, they fell madly in love and Greg was happier than he had ever been in his life.

They were married for three years when Page was diagnosed with pancreatic cancer. She died five months later and Greg was devastated by her loss. But during those wonderful years of their marriage, Greg and Paige were introduced to the Lord's gospel and baptized into His church, and Greg was slowly able to heal from the pains of the past. Apart from marrying his wife, nothing else had ever felt so right.

During his third year of marriage, Greg had been called to be the president of his small branch, a calling that both blew him away and intimidated him because he felt so inadequate and unworthy. Despite his feelings of inadequacy, however, he served with his counselors as faithfully as he could, including during his time of grief, and he loved the members as much or more than they loved him.

Though his calling has kept him busy, the past few years have been full of loneliness and longing for . . .

He supposes he longs for what could have been.

Drawing his thoughts back to the present, Greg kneels by his desk and once again pours out his heart in prayer. He needs direction.

And he will stay on his knees for as long as it takes.

The hours pass and it is almost midnight when he finally hears it.

All will be well, comes the Father's soft voice.

As a comforting warmth surrounds Greg, he covers his face and weeps.

Two Months Later

Greg heaves a deep sigh as he pulls his truck into Salt Lake City. Of all the places he imagined moving to one day, Utah had not been one of them. Oh, he'd wanted to come for a visit sometime and see all the church history that fills the city, but he had never imagined living here for any amount of time. Greg had had many plans for the future, but any plans he had changed with his release as bishop three weeks ago. It had not been unexpected, and it had been time. Maybe that is why he had been so restless, and why God chose the evening of his release to answer his prayers and direct his path. He had asked God to show him the way, to help him know how else he could help build His kingdom.

Heavenly Father's soft answer had come. He has come to recognize the voice well over the last few months.

Help my people in Salt Lake City. Only by losing your life there in my service will you truly find it. Urgency was impressed.

So Greg closed his shop, referred his regular customers to a fellow mechanic he trusted, rented an apartment in Salt Lake (he'd prayed about that as well) packed up what he needed, and left.

Now he will live by heavenly promptings, no longer planning or scheduling his days. His time will no longer be his own.

It will be God's.

J. Adams

Chapter 4

I am always amazed at God's ways. We have been taught that His ways are not ours, and no matter what happens, He is still in charge. I am as sure of that truth as I am of anything, and I relish it.

Adagio St. John's Journal

$\mathcal{I}$t is a very early Sunday morning when our bedroom door cracks open and Dagio sticks his head in.

"Mama, Papa, are you awake?"

"We are now," Adagio answers sleepily and I snort softly.

"Come on in, honey," I tell him. We need to be getting up anyway to get ready for church. Dagio gets into our bed, squirming under the sheet between us. I run my fingers through his soft curls, unruly from sleep.

"I had a dream."

"What did you dream?" Adagio asks.

"I dreamed about Jesus."

Adagio reaches over and squeezes my hand.

"Tell us about it," I urge him. My voice is almost a whisper, my heart racing as a familiar reverent warmth surrounds us.

"He said He loves our family, and that no matter what, He will be with me, and you and Papa. He promised."

"What did you say?" Adagio asks.

"I said I believed Him. Then He hugged me and I woke up."

For a brief moment, we say nothing, each of us immersed in thought. That we believe our son is without question. He has always been very perceptive and sensitive to spiritual things. There have been many times in the past when he has seen those who are unseen, both good and evil spirits, and he has always been comforted enough by the good ones to not be too disturbed by the others. It was from him that we truly learned the reality of spirits being all around us.

Caressing his hair, I tell him, "The Lord is always mindful of us and will see us through whatever comes. If He promised you, then He will keep that promise. Okay?"

"Okay."

"Is there anything else you want to talk about?" Adagio asks.

"No, I just wanted to tell you that."

"We're glad you did."

"I love you, Papa."

"I love you too."

He wraps his arms around me. "I love you, Mama."

Kissing his brow, I say, "I love you too. Now let's get you some breakfast and get ready for church."

Dagio grins and bounces out of bed and quickly heads downstairs to eat. We keep a supply of his favorite frosted wheat cereal and he usually wolfs down a couple of bowls before I even get the eggs done. He definitely has a healthy appetite. I get up and put on a robe and Adagio pulls on some shorts.

"You know," he says, "no matter how many times it happens to us, it still amazes me."

"Me too."

He draws me into his arms and I bury my face against his neck. I love the way he smells. No matter the time of day, his smell is always irresistible. "Do you think God will tell us why we are here soon?" I ask.

"When it is time," he answers, pulling me further into himself. "We will know when it is time."

As Adagio and I sit down in Sunday school class, he tells me there are a lot of empty seats, which is expected since sacrament meeting attendance today was so low. Normally it could be attributed to people being out of town for the holidays, but according to Rand, Adagio's home teaching companion and our ward clerk, attendance has slowly been declining for a while now. That thought saddens me. With the state of the world, we all need God in our lives more now than ever. Yet somehow, many can't seem to see that, or they choose not to.

Today, however, we actually have a new person in the class and he is invited to introduce himself.

"Hi," he says. "I'm Greg Larsen. I just moved here this week from Georgia."

"Well, welcome," the teacher says. "We're glad to have you here."

Greg is sitting right behind us and Adagio and I turn around and whisper hello. He returns our greeting.

When church is over, we visit with Greg for a few minutes and invite him to dinner. He graciously accepts. We know how hard it can be moving to a new place and not knowing anyone, and I am looking forward to finally having a dinner guest. He will be our first since moving to Utah.

Greg follows us home and we sit and visit for a bit before moving to the dining room to eat. Adagio had prepared a crockpot meal this morning and I baked rolls yesterday and bought ice-cream for dessert. I had already set the table before we left for church. I grab an extra setting for our guest.

After Dagio blesses the food, we ask Greg to tell us about himself.

"I'm not used to talking about myself much. What would you like to know?"

"What do you do?" Adagio asks.

"Well, I'm a mechanic and I own an auto shop back in Atlanta."

"I'll be that kept you busy," I say, pouring some juice in a cup for Dagio.

"It did."

"Did you sell it?" Adagio asks.

"No, I just closed up shop and sent my regular customers to a fellow mechanic that I trust."

"So, your move here is not permanent?" I ask, feeling a little disappointed for some reason.

"At the moment, I don't know."

"Well, hopefully the ward will put you to work and you will get a calling." Adagio says. "So far, other than visiting and home teaching, neither of us have received one."

"You never know. But I think I will actually enjoy the break. I was released as bishop almost a month ago."

"Wow!" I say. "I'm sure you were a great one."

"I tried to be," he says humbly.

"Do you have family back in Georgia?" Adagio asks.

"No. My mother died when I was sixteen and I never knew my father, nor my grandparents."

I am saddened by his words and instantly curious. "Forgive me for prying, but where did you live after your mother passed away?"

As Greg shares his impoverished childhood and how he lived on the streets after he lost his mother, I literally ache inside. Though I was adopted as a baby, part of me does understand and I feel for him. That he made it through it and overcame it all to have a successful business of his own and become such a strong person is both amazing and a small miracle. He must have come into the world with a strong spirit.

"Did you ever marry?" I ask.

For a moment, Greg is quiet. When he finally answers, there is a hint of pain in his voice.

"Yes, I did. She passed away a few years ago. Pancreatic cancer. We were only married three years and were unable to have a child before she died."

"I'm so sorry," I softly say and Adagio squeezes my hand.

"Thank you. It has been rough, but thanks to the good Lord, I'm making it."

"Amen," Adagio says. "I guess moving here is a chance to make a fresh start."

"It is."

"Well, we're glad you're here."

"Thank you. So am I." I can hear the smile in his voice. "So tell me a little about you two," Greg prompts. "Your accent sounds Italian. Am I right?"

Adagio chuckles. "You're right, though Evangeline is originally from here. Five years living in Italy and she sounds like a native."

For the next few minutes, we share how we met here in downtown Salt Lake, then married and moved to Italy. Greg's voice is filled with curious awe as he asks about the country and why we moved back to the U.S.

Squeezing my hand, Adagio says, "We just felt like we needed to come back, sort of a prompting."

"I understand," Greg says. "We definitely need to heed those."

When we are done with dinner, Greg offers to help clean up, but we assure him we can handle it, so

Dagio takes him to the family room and keeps him entertained while we put everything away. By the time we join them, Dagio has Greg on the floor with him, indulging in one of his favorite past times, Lego building. Adagio joins them and soon a building contest begins. Dagio is thoroughly enjoying himself and I enjoy listening to the three of them, the two men sounding like young boys one minute then like professional architects the next.

Time slips away and the evening grows late. By the time we walk Greg to the door, we feel like we have known him forever. We invite him back for dinner again in a couple of days and he accepts. Before saying goodbye, he hugs us both and thanks us for our friendship, telling us it means more than he can possibly say. For some reason, I give in to the urge to hug him again.

"Thanks again, Greg," I say, squeezing his hand. "We will see you soon. After all, we have to do our part and keep you sufficiently fed."

He chuckles. "I'll see you."

Adagio closes the door and pulls me close. "A second hug, huh?" he teases. "Do I have competition now?"

I laugh. "Well, I don't know. What does he look like?"

"Tall, dark and handsome with some streaks of gray. Hazel eyes."

"Taller than you?" I ask with a coy smile.

"Maybe a half inch shorter."

"Built?" I run my hands over his muscular chest and arms.

"He's fit."

"Hmmm." I tap a finger against my cheek. "I think I'll pass." Wrapping my arms around his waist, I kiss the corner of his mouth. "Nothing could compare with perfection."

"Nothing?" he breathes huskily before covering my mouth with his.

Nothing.

Greg

Still satisfied from the delicious meal prepared by Adagio and Evangeline, Greg takes a moment to relax on his apartment balcony. The old Avenues home was remodeled last year and converted into four separate apartments, each with its own outside entrance and covered parking space. It is beautiful and reminds him of the apartment above his auto shop after his wife worked her magic on the place, transforming it into a real home for the first time in all the years he'd lived there.

Leaning back in the chair, Greg ponders the wonderful day he'd enjoyed with the St. Johns. As he watches the sun go down over the city, he thinks about the little family and the kindness they showed him. Adagio and Evangeline make a striking couple, and their little boy looks just like his father.

When Adagio and Evangeline first greeted Greg this morning, he had no idea Evangeline was blind, and it wasn't until he'd put his hand out to shake hers in acceptance of their dinner invitation that he realized. He had felt a bit embarrassed, but Adagio had simply smiled and graciously shrugged it off.

Greg couldn't believe how comfortable he felt with them, and he really enjoyed getting to know them. There were some things that he didn't feel the need to share and he chose not to. Maybe once he got to know them better, he would have a desire to, but not right now. He still feels shame when thinking of his past choices, even after all this time, and he wonders if that shame will ever go away. Maybe one day.

For now, he will cherish the new friendship and be grateful. He will also concentrate on discovering and understanding why God led him here.

What is thy will, Father? What would thou have me do? Please show me.

It isn't until Greg awakens in the middle of the night that he is given his answer.

Three hours later, he has a backpack filled, and he is showered, dressed and out the door before the sun rises.

"Show me the way, Father," he prays as he puts the vehicle in gear and drives off.

After driving for two hours, Greg pulls to the side of the canyon road and parks beneath some overhanging trees. Putting on the backpack, he begins the long hike, being guided by the Spirit in the way he should go.

One hour merges into the next and he stops a

couple of times to take a drink of water and eat a granola bar. As he climbs a steep part of the passage, he can't help being grateful for the hiking activities he went on with the youth when he was a bishop. Of course, he has always been active, walking two miles a day and biking five miles on the weekends, but the youth activities helped to prepare him for today.

It is noon by the time he reaches the clearing. As he emerges from the trees, a small group of busy men and women turn toward him. In the distance, there are others emerging from the woods on the opposite side, carrying boxes to a massive tent. One of the men, an older gentleman, leaves the group and walks out to greet him.

"Brother Larsen," the man says with a smile, holding his hand out, catching Greg by surprise. He took the man's hand. "We've been expecting you."

J. Adams

Chapter 5

"Not my will, but thine, be done." *Those were the greatest and most empowering words ever spoken.*

Adagio St. John's Journal

"*I* have decided to sell the company." Mom's announcement comes as a major surprise.

"Really? I thought the company was doing so well now."

"It is. In fact, we've been so successful, I was made an offer by an old rival. Everything inside me is telling me to take it. I prayed about it and the feeling was even stronger."

"Then I guess you should sell."

"I have also been thinking about serving a temple mission."

"Really?" I cry, excited. "Oh, Mom, I think that's an awesome idea!"

"Oh, good. Because I have an appointment with my bishop this evening. Although, with things the way they are in the world, I wonder how much longer before they will have to call the missionaries home."

"Hopefully, not for a little while yet."

"I hope so too. I'm really looking forward to serving."

"You will be wonderful."

Mother plays with Dagio for a while, then heads back to her office to make the call and accept the offer. She promises to call me and let me know how it goes, as well as share the outcome of the meeting with her bishop.

I have just put Dagio to bed when Greg stops by. We haven't talked to him since Sunday. He brings us some pastries from my favorite Italian bakery and thanks us again for dinner. Despite his protests, we decide to make each Wednesday and Sunday a standing dinner date.

"I don't want to put you out," he says.

"You're not putting us out," Adagio assures him.

"And just give up," I tell him. "You're not getting out of it."

He laughs and says, "Okay, okay, you win," finally giving in. "Your wife is very persuasive, Adagio."

"I know. Which is why I can never say no to her."

"Is that a good thing?"

"Well . . ."

"I'm right here, guys," I say and they laugh.

"Thank you," Greg says, his voice sobering. "Your friendship means more than I can say."

I smile, reaching out for his hand and he gives mine a squeeze. "The feeling is mutual. We'll see you tomorrow."

Just before we go to bed, Mom calls. She says the company will be sold in a week. She feels good about her decision and so do we.

Her meeting with her bishop went well, but after some pondering and prayer, she has decided that instead of a temple mission, she is going to pray about where she can be of service and just go and help out wherever God chooses. I am so proud of her for her faith. She promises to keep us posted.

This know also, that in the last days perilous times shall come. For men shall be lovers of their own selves, covetous, boasters, proud, blasphemers, disobedient to parents, unthankful, unholy, Without natural affection, trucebreakers, false accusers, incontinent, fierce, despisers of those that are good, Traitors, heady, highminded, lovers of pleasures more than lovers of God;

2 Timothy 3:1-4

Chapter 6

As prophesied, Salt Lake City truly is among the wicked cities now.

The classification is well deserved.

Adagio St. John's Journal

$\mathcal{S}$o much can change in a year.

I am no longer able to take Dagio out for our neighborhood walks or even to the park without Adagio because it is not as safe as it once was. Especially for me, a blind woman.

The last time we went for a walk, it was to Greg's place just around the block. We were taking him some cookies Dagio helped me make. Adagio was away helping to repair a member's roof. Dagio and I visited with Greg for a while and we had lunch on his balcony. When we finally said goodbye and began our walk back home, Greg caught up with us, took my arm and walked us home. When we got there he told me that there had been a couple of rough-looking young men standing on the corner smoking and he had been concerned for our safety. I was grateful to him for watching out for us. As much as I miss my independence, we don't go anywhere alone.

Laws are constantly being passed to favor various groups while infringing on the rights of others. Tolerance is preached by some, but those same people don't live it themselves. I discovered long ago that tolerance is a conditional word and does not bear the same meaning it once did, at least where we humans are concerned.

Crime has gone up, making me grateful for the gun Adagio purchased last year. I am also grateful for the two years' worth of food lining the shelves of our storage room. For decades, Church leaders have urged the members to have sufficient food storage in the event of an emergency. They knew there would come a day that we would need it, and it is clear to anyone reading the signs that that time is not far off. There is also a vast amount of food storage in the villa in Italy. Phillip and Mali have been diligent in keeping the rotation going and making sure nothing spoils.

Earthquakes, tsunamis, tornadoes, and volcanic eruptions abound, and we frequently check the forecasts in both this country and Italy since all of our family is there.

Thinking of home, I smile. After much praying about where to go and serve, Mom had received her answer. Italy. She has been staying with my in-laws for almost a year, spending her days with them, helping with church work and serving the members in any way she can. Phillip and Mali stay pretty busy and they love having her there to help.

When we are not schooling Dagio or helping in church work, I work on my personal family history. Mom has been doing hers and she shared the information with me to fill in my records. We also worked on Father's and managed to go back quite a ways. But Mom knew I needed more than that. I needed to know where I came from.

She provided the name of my biological mother, including some birth information, and with Adagio's help, I managed to get back several generations. Though I don't know any more about Althea Hines, my biological mother, I have felt her near, and I look forward to meeting her one day. I have no idea what led her to such a sad end, but she must have experienced some hard things.

Unfortunately, I haven't been able to find anything on my biological father. His name was not listed on the hospital records. He is a ghost and I have no idea if he is even alive. Was he a drug addict too? Did he even know I existed? I have no way of knowing, and short of a miracle, I will probably never know.

With all the adversity in the world, I still give thanks throughout each day. I have a wonderful life and there is still some good to be found. Tender mercies abound and God's hand is apparent everywhere I turn. It is good to know He is still in control.

Greg has become like a member of the family. In fact, when he isn't working his construction job in

Ogden Canyon, he spends so much time with us, Dagio has taken to calling him 'Grandpa Greg.' The first time Dagio called him that, Adagio had laughed because Greg's surprised expression was so priceless. Now he is completely used to it and totally dotes on Dagio, bringing him little treats or small gifts whenever he comes over. And he never fails to bring my favorite pastries.

"You're spoiling us," I said one day.

"Nothing wrong with that," he replied. "I've never had family to spoil before."

That single statement said so much. I hugged him and thanked him for being such an amazing person and he actually got a little emotional. Then Adagio hugged him and Dagio finally wrapped his arms around his neck and said, "I love you, Grandpa Greg."

Looking back now, I can see how much our son had needed a grandfather in his life. Of course, no one will ever take the place of Grandpa Phillip, and we Skype with Phillip, Mali and Mom every other Sunday. It makes being away from them a little easier.

Greg

One afternoon, Greg stops by and finds Adagio mowing the front lawn.

"Hey," Adagio says, turning off the mower. "The weather is cooling so fast, this may be one of the last times I have to mow this year."

"Yeah, I know Utah has strange weather, but this is kind of weird." Greg had gotten used to the unpredictability of the weather here, but this cold front was definitely unexpected. "I don't mean to interrupt you."

"You're not. Go on inside. Dagio is upstairs reading and Evangeline is out visiting teaching, but . . . she made a coconut cake."

Greg grins. "My favorite! How did she know?"

Adagio smirks. "I have no idea."

Greg laughs, loving Adagio's sense of humor.

"Go have some. Just let me finish this small bit and I will be in."

"Sounds good."

Greg goes inside and makes his way to the kitchen, helping himself to a piece of Evangeline's homemade coconut cake. As he sits down to eat, he ponders Evangeline. Despite not having her sight, she is a very accomplished woman. She is a brilliant musician and he loves hearing her play, whether it's the piano, violin, cello, or rocking out on the drums. And the woman can cook better than most sighted people, with the exception of her husband. The man truly is a master chef, as well as a gifted musician in his own right.

Greg has never seen a better or more loving mother than Evangeline, and it is obvious that she and Adagio are madly in love with each other. He counts himself both blessed and fortunate to be in their lives.

"Enjoying the cake?" Adagio asks, entering the kitchen, his eyes filled with amusement.

"You know it. Is there anything Evangeline can't do?"

"Well, she would state the obvious, but being blind has never stopped her from doing anything."

Adagio

Pushing his plate aside, Greg says, "If you don't mind me asking, how long has she been blind?"

"Don't mind at all and she would not either."

Adagio loves talking about his wife. It is one of his favorite things to do. "Evangeline was born blind. She has always been able to see light and shadows and muted colors, but that is it."

"She must have had amazing parents to raise her to be so independent."

Adagio pauses before speaking again. "We consider you family, so I will share a little about my wife's upbringing."

"Will she mind?"

"Not at all. It is what made her who she is. First of all, Evangeline was adopted when she was a baby. Her mother was an addict and drank and did drugs during her pregnancy, which is the reason Evangeline was born blind. It is a miracle that she suffered no other health problems. Apparently her mother died of an overdose right after Evangeline was delivered. There was no father in the picture so she was turned over to the state. George and Kathryn Patton came along and immediately filed adoption papers. Evangeline told me that when she became an adult and was finally on her own, she came to realize that their adopting her was purely philanthropic, and though they gave her all the material things money could buy, they did not give her love."

Greg continues to quietly listen as Adagio shares what he had overheard Evangeline's adopted father say to her while he was hiding in another room. Evangeline had told him how cold the man was and Adagio had the chance to actually hear his vile words.

"I need to talk to you," her father said, pushing past her. He was obviously drunk.

"Father, this isn't a good time for me right now."

"Well, it's the perfect time for me." There was no kindness in his voice. "Thanks to your coldness, the Tanners are pulling out of the deal."

"I'm sorry the merger fell through, but I am not to blame."

"Oh, you better believe you are. But I'm about to tell you how you will make it up to me. My new perspective partner has a penchant for you so-called women of color. It's about time you earned the good life I've provided for you. Just keep him happy until we seal the deal. Who knows, you might grow to like it and want to make it permanent. This is what I have been grooming you for, Evangeline. And since

you can't see the man, it shouldn't make a difference what he looks like."

Evangeline shook, hurt and anger filling her features. Her father placed no value on his daughter. Other than being the Mercury Technologies company whore, she wasn't worth much else in his eyes. "Does Mother know about this?"

"I don't answer to your mother. I am the head of my house. My word is law, so she has no choice but to support me. Besides, I take care of her well enough."

"Adopted or not, I am still your daughter. How can you treat me this way?"

"Because I own you, that's how. And a good daughter would be obedient and not give me any lip."

She slipped her shaking hands into the pockets of her jeans. "Father, I would like you to leave now." She tried to keep her voice calm. "And please don't come back." His anger increased and she moved back.

"I will leave when I am good and ready! Who do you think you are, the African Queen or something? It is because of me you even have all of this." He swung his arms around the living room. "Do you really think you can order me around like some whipping boy? If you do, then think again. I guess I'm going to have to show you who is in charge."

Before his hand could make contact with Evangeline's face, Adagio caught his arm, spinning him around. "I wouldn't do that if I were you." His voice was icy and he watched her father's eyes widen.

"Who the hell are you and what are you doing in my daughter's apartment?"

"I am Evangeline's friend, and why I am here is none of your business." He glanced at Evangeline. "Are you all right?" When she tearfully nodded, his piercing eyes move back to her father. "I suggest you leave now. Or do you need a little help?"

Her father slowly smiled. "Oh, I see how it is. Sleeping with her, are you? You're not the first, you know?"

An emotional gasp escaped Evangeline. "How can you say something like that?"

"Well it's true, isn't it? And I'm sure your foreign playboy here can teach you something new. Your experience will come in handy for Mercury. I can put you both on the payroll."

"Get out!" she yelled. "Just get out!"

He moved toward her. "Why you little tramp! I'll . . ."

In two swift moves, Adagio had the man's arms

twisted behind his back. "You are seriously delusional. Not just delusional, you are sick."

"Get your hands off me!"

"I will," Adagio said, yanking him toward the door. "Evangeline, would you mind?" She nervously moved to the door and quickly opened it. Releasing her father's arms, Adagio pitched him against the hallway wall and slammed the door shut.

"Evangeline was an emotional mess afterward and I moved her in with me that night, in this very house in fact. About a week later, Evangeline's mother called and said her father was in the hospital on life support. He was driving drunk and hit someone head on. He didn't live past that day. Her mother also had a softening of the heart and began to make amends that day as well." Adagio pauses, his love for Evangeline filling him with a familiar warmth that only she can produce. "I married an amazing woman."

"Can I ask how old she is?" Greg's voice is soft, almost timid.

"She's thirty-three."

"A philanthropic trip, huh? Where did they

adopt her from?"

"I believe it was Georgia."

Adagio notices a pained look briefly fill Greg's eyes, but in an instant, it is gone.

"She really has been through some trials."

There is emotion in Greg's voice and tears mist his eyes, and Adagio is touched by his compassion. He is grateful for the close friendship they have developed. "She has, but as I said, her trials made her who she is. If you asked her, I know she would tell you she would not change a thing."

Greg nods, but says nothing.

"Hey, *bella*," Adagio says as Evangeline and Dagio enter the kitchen.

"Grandpa Greg!" Dagio immediately launches himself into Greg's arms and Greg laughs.

"How you doing, bud?"

"Good. You want to build Legos with me?"

"I wish I could, but I have to go. But I will on Sunday, okay?"

"Okay," Dagio agrees, disappointment in his voice.

"Hey," Adagio says, "I will play with you. I

know I'm not as much fun as Grandpa Greg, but . . ."

"You *are*, Papa."

His earnestness makes Adagio smile. "Okay, you go on up and I will be there." He stands to kiss his wife. "How was your visit?"

"It was great. Nell is having surgery tomorrow and I volunteered us to bring dinner in for her family."

"Sounds good."

Greg stands abruptly. "I need to go. I appreciate the cake, Evangeline."

"You're welcome. Can't you say a little longer?"

"I can't. But we'll visit Sunday, okay?"

"All right. I'll walk you to the door," she says, reaching out for his arm in her usual way, but he takes her hand instead.

"Good to see you, Greg," Adagio says. "I'm heading up to do some construction with Dagio."

"Good to see you too, and thanks for the visit. See you Sunday."

Greg

Greg squeezes Evangeline's hand as they walk to the door, his thoughts running a mile a minute, as well as his heart. When they reach the door, he finds himself just staring at her. He can't help it. He feels tears threatening again and manages to hold them back.

"Thanks again for the cake, Evangeline. You're a great cook." He struggles to keep the growing emotion from his voice.

"Well, I figured since coconut cake was your favorite, the least I could do was learn to make it."

"That means a lot to me."

"Are you okay?" Evangeline asks.

Greg swallows hard. "I'm good. I have to go. I'll see you."

"Okay."

He embraces her, doing his best not to hold onto her. He quickly releases her and leaves.

Greg manages to hold himself together, but as soon as he is inside his apartment, like the fury of a hurricane, a storm of emotion hits hard and fast, the force of it bringing him to his knees.

She has Althea's eyes. Althea's smile, and I never saw it.

"Oh, Father, this is why you brought me here. I

prayed to do thy will and to somehow make amends for the choice I made so long ago, and you answered both prayers. Oh, Father, Father, help me."

Greg immediately feels the warm embrace of the Savior and hears His voice.

Tell her.

"Oh, Lord, how do I tell her? She's been through so much. It will hurt her."

She is strong and possesses a heart of unconditional love.

"I'm so sorry I abandoned her."

I have paid the price for you. You have carried the burden, but I have carried you.

"When should I tell her?"

You will know the time.

"And you will be with me?"

I have never left your side.

"Did Greg seem okay to you?" I ask Adagio as we get ready for bed.

"He seemed a little out of it. I wonder if hearing your story upset him a bit. I assured him that you are stronger because of what you went through. It shows how connected he has become to our little family."

"I think I'll give him a call tomorrow."

We kneel and pray before getting into bed. The day had been unexpectedly cool, but the night is a chilly one. I am cold, but Adagio is always my private furnace, and lying in his arms quickly warms me.

"Today, Linda and I found out that two more stores in the mall have closed," I tell him. "A few of the ward members lost their jobs and are struggling."

Adagio sighs. "So many businesses are struggling right now and unemployment just keeps going up. That is why having food storage is so important. It is an inspired admonishment."

"I sometimes feel a little guilty that we have so much when others have so little, but I am grateful."

"So am I. Let's talk to the bishop and see what we can do to help."

I smile, kissing him, grateful that he is always thinking of others. "Okay."

He kisses me again and turns off the lamp."

Just on the edge of sleep, Adagio murmurs, "But the best thing we can do is pray for this country, and the world."

A month later, the economy collapses and the country truly begins to fall apart.

Chapter 7

Without the Lord, we are nothing.
But to the Lord, we are everything.
Adagio St. John's Journal

$\mathscr{C}$hristmas Day is subdued as the nation tries to come to grips with its current state. But in our home, there is peace as we remember the birth of the Savior and celebrate His life. As far as gifts, we only give things that truly matter.

To Dagio, we give a set of leather scriptures engraved with his name and a couple of illustrated books of Bible stories. Because he has become such a reader, he is absolutely pleased with them. To Adagio, I give some doctrinal books. I give some to Greg as well. From Adagio I receive a new set of braille scriptures and a new journal to replace the one I recently filled. Greg gives Adagio a book of quotes by church leaders and Dagio some puzzles. He tells me my gift will be a little late and he will bring it over tomorrow. He apologizes and I assure him it is okay.

After a wonderful Christmas dinner, we Skype with the family and introduce them to Greg. They are all pleased to meet him and tell him they look forward to seeing him in person one day.

As we visit, I can tell Phillip is impressed with Greg, which is important to me. I can't explain why I feel such a strong need for the family to accept him, nor can I explain why I have begun to need him close. Maybe it is a deep-seated longing for some kind of father figure in my life. I love Adagio's father very much, but with Greg it goes deeper, a fact that is kind of jarring since I only met the man last year. But his presence has made the past year complete somehow.

After we end our call, Greg stays a while longer, putting together a puzzle with Dagio.

When he is finally ready to leave, he kisses my cheek and promises to see me in the morning.

Greg

When Greg gets home, he immediately kneels by his bed and prays harder than he has ever prayed in his life. He is so afraid of what he must do, but he knows he can't wait any longer or let fear rule him.

How many times in the past had he wished he could go back and change what he did? How many days had he longed to change the destructive choices he'd made? Because one choice had led to another and the emotional consequences have been great.

When Greg was told by Adagio what Evangeline had dealt with before they met, he felt his heart break. She had been treated horribly by the man who raised her as his daughter. And Greg blamed himself. It he had gone to the hospital the night of Evangeline's birth and accepted his responsibility, she would have been spared such treatment. No, he would not have been able to give her all the things her adopted parents did, but he could have given her love. That would've been more important than any material thing he could have given her.

Now Greg has been given the opportunity to ask for his daughter's forgiveness and really know her *as* his daughter. He only prays that she will find it in her heart to give him a chance–a chance to be her father.

"Bless me with the strength to do this, Father," he pleads. "Please."

You have the strength. And the courage. You will not be alone.

Internalizing the warm answer, Greg goes to bed early, completely exhausted emotionally. He drifts to sleep with a continued prayer in his heart, and on his lips, that Evangeline will forgive him.

Adagio gets a call from a neighbor and is asked to come and help give a priesthood blessing to their sick daughter. While he is gone, I read Dagio a bedtime story from one of my braille storybooks and get him settled in bed. Deciding to wait for Adagio, I make a mug of chocolate and sit in the large leather chair in the family room. Closing my eyes, I rest my head against the back of the chair and ponder the day.

Truthfully, this has been the most spiritual

Christmas season I have ever experienced. There had been no running to and fro trying to find that perfect gift. No swimming through crowds of people and waiting in mile-long lines. We had given thought to how we would celebrate months ago and purchased gifts accordingly. We spent yesterday and the day before baking treats and delivering them to neighbors. And we loaded our SUV with groceries and took them to the homeless shelter.

Yes, it has been a simple yet joyous day with our thoughts centered completely on Christ. It's been perfect. I sigh, happiness and contentment filling me, and continue to ponder. The ticking of the clock plays a soft rhythm in the silence, my body and mind growing languid with each tick.

A moment later, the dim room is suddenly filled with light and He appears before me. I smile, my vision perfect once again.

"My Lord," I whisper, immediately kneeling.

He takes my hand in His, smiling back, his eyes full of love. I raise my eyes and open His hands, again taking in the nail prints in His palms. Helping me up and guiding me to the sofa, He sits down next to me.

"Evangeline, do you have faith in me?"

"Yes, Lord. You know my heart."

"I do. Just as you know me." It wasn't a question, but I nod anyway. He softly admonishes, "Then look."

I feel as if I am suddenly transported to another place and am no longer in my body. The scene my eyes behold is indescribable, too great and terrible to put into words.

I see a massive earthquake ripping apart Salt Lake City, as well as other cities in the United States. I see fighting and looting, disease and death. Men, women and children killing each other without thought. People dying in the streets from an illness that has no cure.

I witness the country being invaded by foreign militaries. I see God's righteous indignation and destruction of the earth and all the wicked upon it. But I also see God's love pouring out upon the righteous during the coming tribulation.

Things I never imagined witnessing with my blind eyes are before me now, the colors vivid, the images containing a richness that only reality can bring.

Then the scene changes and I behold the world from its very beginning to its glorious end. From the earth's creation and the placing of Adam and Eve-our first parents-in the Garden of Eden, to Noah and the flood. I witness Moses delivering his people from Egypt, Solomon building the Lord's temple.

I witness the birth of Jesus Christ, his life, death and resurrection. I see the Lord appearing to the ancient inhabitants of North America. I see the apostasy, the gospel being restored through God's chosen prophet.

I am shown so many things that by the time the vision closes, I am completely drained. Then my Lord touches me and my strength is restored. Tears of joy falling down my face, I stare at him in awe.

He squeezes my hand. "Your faith is sure and so are you."

"Oh, Lord, Lord!" is all I can say, my heart is so full, my spirit on fire.

"You need to leave, Evangeline. Adagio will know where."

"But how will . . ." As soon as I begin to ask, I know the answer. "You will go to Him. He will see you."

"He will. There is a great work for your family to do."

I smile, tears filling my eyes again. "I love you, Lord."

"And I love you." Placing a warm hand on my cheek, He says, "Close your eyes, Evangeline." I immediately comply and He covers my eyes with His hand. His final words are a whisper that will echo in my mind forever.

"Be healed."

Adagio

Walking up the sidewalk to his home, a strong prompting draws Adagio to the back yard. Not understanding why, he makes his way through the dark to the porch, sits in one of the wicker chairs and waits. Seconds later, there is a bright light, and the Savior appears before him. As He approaches, Adagio drops to his knees.

"Touch me," comes His loving voice, and Adagio does so, pressing his fingers against the nail prints in Christ's hands.

Awed and overwhelmed, Adagio lowers his head, resting his brow on the Savior's feet. "My Lord."

Taking his hand and lifting him up, the Lord asks, "Adagio, do you have faith in me?"

"Yes, Lord. You know all things and can see into my heart." When the Savior smiles, Adagio is immersed in warmth and love.

"Then look."

I hear the door open and my heart threatens to pound right through my chest. In the last few minutes, my emotions have run the gamut.

I can see!

When I had opened my eyes, the Savior was no longer standing before me, but I felt Him near as the clarity of my vision grew and expanded, taking in everything at once. Everything was new, yet familiar, as if I knew what every object my eyes fell upon was, I had only briefly forgotten what they looked like.

I had walked the perimeter of the family room, touching object after object–the clock on the wall, the Italian masks and figurines on the mantle, the television and remote, the curtains hanging from the large window. And finally, the piano. I lightly ran my hand across the shiny black surface, sat on the bench and touched the keys that my fingers knew so well.

Then I picked up the silver frame bearing a photograph of me, Adagio and Dagio. I touched the glass, tears immediately brimming my eyes and spilling down my cheeks. Our little boy looks just like his father.

My beautiful family.

My thoughts return to the present as Adagio enters the room. Judging by the tears on his face, the Savior had come to him.

"Stay where you are," I softly say, startling him. Then I walk to him, my eyes never breaking contact with his, his eyes growing wider with each step I take. When I reach him, I slowly lift my hand to his face and gently cup his wet cheek. My hand moves to his hair and I caress the thick black locks hanging well past his collar. His emerald eyes are green pools as they stare into mine. I let my hands drift down to his chest and travel over his biceps before trailing down and resting on his waist.

"Oh, angel!" he breathes.

"You are beautiful," I whisper just as his lips come down on mine, his moist, heated mouth plying mine in abandon. He kisses me like there is no tomorrow and I answer his powerful affections with the voraciousness of my own. On and on we kiss, never stopping to draw a breath, never needing to. For a moment, I open my eyes during the kiss, just to look at him and he does the same. I don't think I will ever stop wanting to look at him.

Sweeping me up in his arms, Adagio carries me into the small den just off the family room and kicks the door shut. Passion resumes as we love like we never have before, and I take all he gives, giving back in equal measure.

A long while later, our affections soften, our swollen lips finally parting with Adagio's whispered, "Come and see what I see when I look at you."

Putting our discarded clothes back on, we walk upstairs to our bedroom, my feet and senses automatically knowing the way.

Leading me to the bathroom, Adagio tells me to close my eyes, which I do, until he positions me in front of the vanity mirror. Moving behind me and wrapping his arms around my waist, he says against my ear, "Open your eyes."

As my lids slowly open, I look at the stranger reflected before me and I slowly smile. I touch the thick, auburn hair hanging past my shoulders, the riot of natural curls wild and framing my face like a lion's mane. Laughing light brown eyes stare back at me and full lips frame the mouth that curves into an even wider smile. I take in the light caramel skin on my face and arms, and watch the bumps rise on my skin with the warm touch of Adagio's caressing hands.

"I can't believe this is me," I finally say.

"It's you," Adagio says in amused assurance and a chuckle bubbles from inside me.

For a few minutes, we just stand there, Adagios arms firmly wrapped around me, my hands pressed against his, his head resting against mine, and we continue to stare at our reflection. Over and over, a prayer of thanks runs through my mind, gratitude exploding inside me for everything I have experienced this night. My testimony of Heavenly Father and Jesus Christ has been solid for a long time, but as the Savior affirmed, my faith is perfect and I know now without a doubt that He *is*. I don't just believe, I *know*.

"He came to you," I softly state.

"He did, *amore*," Adagio says, pressing his face into my hair. "He is magnificent!"

"He is."

"We have to leave."

"I know." I turn to face him, looking into his eyes. "When?"

"Now."

Chapter 8

We are promised that the Lord will not forsake us in our tribulation as long as we remain faithful. Those who question His ways are not always ready for His answer. 'Thy will be done' should not be just uttered words.

Adagio St. John's Journal

With solemn yet hopeful hearts, we drive away from the beautiful home we inherited from my husband's grandparents, never looking back, only forward.

For many, it will be hard to leave their home, knowing they will never see it again.

Not so for us.

The problem with humans is we get so caught up in *things,* so attached to material possessions that we forget what is really important–what is *most* important.

When Adagio told me we needed to leave immediately, I did not question it. I just knew it must be so. We had showered and changed and packed one large suitcase, fitting what was necessary for the three of us. I also added the books Dagio got for Christmas. Adagio grabbed our 72-hour kits from the storage room–to which I added our scriptures–and told me arrangements would be made to bring the rest of the food and supplies because they would be needed.

We awakened our son and explained that Heavenly Father wanted us to leave. Dagio asked where we were going and we told him the Lord would lead us. He quickly dressed.

Loading our backpacks, suitcase, thick sleeping bags rolled up in foam mats, and the large, all-weather tent into the vehicle, we turned off all the lights and locked up the house and said a prayer for a safe journey.

Since Adagio was counseled to leave all phones

and electronics (we would not have a signal where we were going anyway) I tearfully text Greg to let him know we left. I don't give him an explanation, I only say we had to leave. I tell him how sorry we are and we hope to see him again. Pushing the "send" button breaks my heart, but there is no choice.

As we drive off, Adagio gives my hand a squeeze.

"Will we see him again?" I ask.

"I don't know, *amore*. If it is God's will."

Please let it be thy will, I silently pray. *Please, Father.*

Then the Savior whispers peace to my heart and my emotions calm.

Greg

The images in Greg's dreams are disturbing and his sleep is uneasy.

Peace, comes the Lord's soft voice, instantly calming him. *Let your mind be at peace. I have a work for you to do. And all will be well.*

Behold, the day of the Lord cometh, cruel both with wrath and fierce anger, to lay the land desolate: and he shall destroy the sinners thereof out of it.

Isaiah 13:9

Chapter 9

Despite what many think, all is not well in Zion.
Adagio St. John's Journal

$\mathcal{T}$he hike up the mountain path is long, and steep in some places, but we keep going, stopping only twice for a drink and a few minutes of rest. Blessedly, there has been a full moon to light our way through the darkness. We each have a pack strapped to our back along with our sleeping bag and mat. I pull the suitcase and Adagio carries the large tent. Sometimes when the suitcase becomes a struggle, he takes it from me and pulls it himself. He is so strong, he is able to do it with no problem. We keep Dagio walking between us. He shoulders his gear without complaint, making me so proud of him.

By the time we crest the hill and emerge from the trees, it is just after six in the morning. My legs and shoulders ache like they never have before and Dagio is almost dead on his feet, but neither of us utter a word of complaint because Adagio had shouldered most of the work. I chastise myself and make a vow to get stronger so I can be a help, not a burden. And judging from the vision the Lord showed me, I will have more than ample opportunity.

It isn't quite light yet and there are lanterns lit in the distance amid several tents. As we make our way across the clearing, someone exits a tent and walks out to greet us.

"Welcome," the older man says. "We're so glad you're here, and that you heeded the prompting."

Ours had been far more than a prompting, but we will never tell, at least, not until God wants us to.

"Thank you," Adagio says. "We are the St. Johns. I am Adagio, this is my wife, Evangeline and our son, young Adagio, but we call him Dagio."

"It's good to meet you. I'm Eban Hunter. I was assigned to preside over this place of refuge."

"It is good to meet you too," Adagio says.

"Follow me and I'll show you where you can set up camp." As we walk, Eban says, "Let me guess, you're from Italy, right?"

"How did you know?" I ask teasingly and he chuckles softly.

"Definitely the accent."

"My husband was born and raised in Italy, but I am originally from Salt Lake. We married over seven years ago and Italy became my home for a while."

"What brought you back?"

Adagio smiles slightly. "We knew we needed to be here."

Eban smiles back. "I understand."

He takes us to a spot just beyond a trio of massive tents set up next to a spacious pavilion.

"These are the food and medical supply tents." He points to a tent a few yards away. "That is mine and my wife's place. She will be up in a bit, but I'm guessing you folks are exhausted and could use some rest."

"That we could," Adagio says.

"I'll let you get set up then. You need any help?"

"No, we should be fine. The tent is pretty easy to set up."

"Well, I'll let you get to it and see you when you wake up. Oh, and there are a couple of portable bathrooms on the other side of the pavilion just through the trees if you need them. There is also a water tank with a spigot."

I nod. "See you later. And thank you."

"No problem at all."

Adagio pulls out the tent, the connecting rods making the setup fast and easy. We had spent quite a bit on the tough and sturdy shelter, but it was worth it. It sleeps eight to ten comfortably, so we will have plenty of room with just the three of us.

Once the tent is set up, we take everything inside and make our beds. Because it is so cold, Dagio sleeps next to me, but our tent still holds the heat in much better than most. It also has a vent in the ceiling for cooking or a small propane heater. We have a stove and a heater stored with the food storage we left. It will be appreciated when it finally arrives.

We all make a quick bathroom run before settling into our sleeping bags. The three of us are cocooned together with Dagio in front of me and Adagio behind me. Adagio and I had zipped our bags together and he holds me snugly against him.

"I love you," I whisper.

"I love you too," he says back, kissing my cheek and tightening his embrace.

We immediately fall into an exhausted sleep.

J. Adams

Chapter 10

The gospel truly is a shelter from the storm.
Adagio St. John's Journal

*W*hen I finally awaken, I am briefly disoriented. Adagio is not beside me, and for a moment I panic. Then I hear the gentle cadence of his heavily-accented voice outside and my heart calms.

Dagio is still snuggled against me and I give in to the urge to caress his dark curls, freshly amazed by how beautiful he is. Trying not to wake him, I slowly sit up. As I do, a wave of nausea instantly hits me and I lay back down. Closing my eyes, I swallow against the rising sickness. Looking up at the ceiling of the tent, my vision blurs as tears trail back into my hair. I have been sick the past couple of days and my period is three weeks late, but because I have been late before, I dared not think too much about it. We have tried for so long to have another baby, and I didn't think it would ever happen. But there is no doubt in my mind now.

My tears are a mixture of joy and worry. I am more grateful than I can say for the blessing of bringing another child into the world, but he or she won't have an easy time of it. None of us will. Dealing with a pregnancy in this situation will be a trial. However it is a trial I will gladly accept. In my heart I know that God knows this. He always has.

Slowly sitting up again, I get out of the sleeping bag, crawl over to my backpack, and fish for a pack of cheese crackers. I eat a few and wash them down with a few sips of water, hoping it will be enough to calm my stomach.

Taking a brush and comb from the backpack, I try to do something with my hair. I end up pulling it up into a loose bun. Having bought a pregnancy test last week, I'd slipped it into my pack before we left the house. I quickly find it and stuff it into my small hygiene bag, put on my shoes, and slip out of the tent.

Adagio is over at the far end of the pavilion right now, taking with Eban and another man. When he looks in my direction, I wave and he says something to the men before quickly making his way over to me.

"*Dolcezza,* how are you feeling?" he asks, taking me in his arms.

"Fine," I say, not wanting to complain. I caress his cheek. "Did you get enough sleep?"

"I did. Eban has been filling me in on everything. I will tell you when you get back."

"Okay."

I make my way to the portable bathroom and take the test, not surprised by the positive result. Now I just worry about how Adagio will take the news. Deep down, I know he will be happy, but I also know he will worry for me and I don't want that. I don't want to be a burden. *There goes my whole 'getting stronger' scenario.*

I quickly wash my face and hands and brush my teeth before making my way back to the tent.

"Where is Dagio?" I ask Adagio. His sleeping bag is rolled up and placed next to the suitcase.

"He is out playing. A new family arrived while we were sleeping. I met them earlier. It is a father with two young children Dagio's age. His name is Dan. His wife left him *and* the church a year ago and never came back. He heeded the prompting to come as well."

"That poor man. This must be so hard for him."

"He said it has been, but it is easy to see he has strong faith. His son and daughter are very sweet, full of the innocent curiosity that comes with being a child."

"I'll have to meet them later. I'm sure we will be meeting new people frequently, at least I hope so." My thoughts suddenly shift to Greg and a profound sadness fills me. What must he have felt when he received my text and read that we left so suddenly? And with no explanation.

All I can do is have faith that we will see him again, if it is God's will. Still, I can't help the sadness I feel. I miss him already. I still don't understand how I can feel so attached to him.

As nausea rolls through my insides again, I experience an emotional spike and I lie on my side, unable to stop the tears from coming.

"Evangeline?" He lays down beside me, taking

me in his arms. "Sweetheart, what is it? What's wrong?"

Drawing back, I caress his face, allowing my gaze to roam over his handsome features. They are still new, yet they are so familiar. Last night I spent so much time staring at him, I now know every line of his face. Every contour. How I love looking at him! I am an emotional mess, yet truly being able to see his beloved face, as well as our son's, brings me an indescribable joy. I continue to touch him, lightly pressing my fingers over his lips. I need to tell him, and there is only one way to do that.

"Adagio . . . I'm pregnant."

Adagio

Various feelings and emotions flow through Adagio's head, but one stands prominently at the forefront of his mind and heart.

Joy!

Absolute and indescribable joy!

Adagio hadn't known if they would ever be blessed with another child. Heavenly Father works on His own timetable, and it seems *now* is the time. He won't question why. He won't give place to fears and the trials they will face, and the fact that it will be doubly hard for Evangeline. He will only concentrate on the fact that they have been given a gift, and be grateful for it."

Adagio stares into his wife's eyes, wiping her tears. "*Amore*, this baby is a gift, one that I will be eternally grateful for. I know it will be hard, but God will be with us. He will be with *you*. As will I." He smiles and draws her close, whispering against her ear, "I'm so happy, angel."

I hold onto my husband, crying against his neck. "Are you really happy?" I ask, drawing back a little.

"Very happy."

"So am I."

And I really am. Deep down I know we will be watched over. The Savior promised me He will always be with me.

And I know with absolute certainty He will carry me through this.

Chapter 11

God knows what we can handle and what we cannot.

So it stands to reason that with *God, there is nothing we cannot handle.*

Adagio St. John's Journal

Throughout the afternoon, I do what I can to help around the camp, saying hello and getting to know the others in the group. And Adagio was right. Dan is a wonderful person and his kids are adorable. I'm so glad Dagio has friends here and will not feel so alone. And hopefully when the official invitation to gather has been extended, there will be many more children here.

I also get to know Eban's wife, Kay. She is a sweet lady who oozes love and has captured the heart of every person here.

Dinnertime is a simple meal of beef stew, biscuits, and Dutch oven cobbler that I help Kay prepare. I am sure we will need more kitchen help once more people begin to arrive. During cleanup, I become a little nauseated, which prompts me to share our baby news with Kay. She is happy for us and gives me a few extra biscuits to take to our tent to nibble on.

Exhaustion finally hits me and I retire to our tent early. I worry about not doing my fair share and promise myself I will get up in the morning when Adagio does. I spread out our sleeping bags, zipping mine and Adagio's together again, then I change into warm pajamas and crawl inside.

But as tired as I feel, I can't seem to shut my mind off. So many thoughts and concerns tumble in my head. About the baby. About our future.

I am no longer worried, but the baby will need so many things. Adagio had packed a pouch of emergency cash, as well as a stash of silver dollar pieces he'd started buying as soon as we moved back to Utah. But without access to things like cloth diapers, blankets, and baby clothes, and even maternity clothing, the money will be useless. Even though I knew before we came that pregnancy was a possibility, I hadn't thought of these things because there had not been time.

Clearing my thoughts, I smile. *Not to worry, the Lord will provide. He always does.* And I figure if the pioneer women could do it, so can I.

"Where are you?" Adagio's voice draws me from my thoughts. He changes into a pair of sweat pants and slips into the sleeping bag behind me, drawing me into his warm embrace.

"I'm here. Just thinking about how bless I am, and how I know God will bless us with what we need."

"He will," he agrees, nuzzling the back of my neck.

"Where's Dagio?" I ask.

"He is with Alicia and Brad. Dan said he would send him back by bedtime."

"Dagio's definitely attached to them."

"I am sure they will be the best of friends

through the coming years. He will need them. They will need each other."

"Do you think many will come?"

"I don't know, *amore*," he sighs. "When the Brethren finally extend the invitation to gather, it will definitely be a test of faith. Many will not want to leave their home and the comforts they are used to. The majority will likely have the mindset that things are good for them now and will want to wait until they think things are bad enough to leave instead of leaving when they are counseled to. By the time they make the choice to leave, it will be far worse for them than if they had listened in the first place. The Father will not turn His back on them, but choices bear consequences and they will lose some of the blessings."

"I pray they will listen."

"I pray for that as well."

For a few moments, we are silent, listening to the sound the camp. The echo of muted voices is soothing.

"I know it has only been a day, but you know what I really miss?" I finally ask.

"Yes," he says, kissing my ear. "Music."

"You, too?"

"*Si, amore.* Me, too."

Dagio finally enters the tent. We turn on the flashlight and spend a few minutes listening to him tell us about his time with Alicia and Brad. Then he changes and we all pray together before he snuggles into his sleeping bag close to me.

Just on the edge of sleep, I murmur to Adagio, "You know what else I miss?"

Tightening his embrace, he murmurs back, "Greg."

Greg.

Chapter 12

Like any loving parent, the Father can only admonish and counsel His children so much. We make our choices and live with them.

Adagio St. John's Journal

Greg

$\mathcal{I}$t is just after dawn when Greg pulls the large white delivery truck up to the tall, barbwire-topped fence protecting the mountain camp. This is opposite the way he entered the very first time he came. Over time he had helped to put up the fence and others continue to extend it. They plan to completely enclose the camp to help protect what will be one of the Lord's celestial cities because it will house some of Heavenly Father's most obedient. How grateful Greg is to be found worthy enough to be included.

Pulling up behind Greg in a minivan is a family of four–a husband and wife and their twin sixteen-year-old son and daughter. The family lived two doors down from Greg's apartment building. The father had received revelation to take his family away and had heeded the prompting.

When Greg woke up to find Evangeline's text, the pain in his heart had been excruciating. He had immediately gotten dressed and rushed over to their place, hoping against hope that maybe it was a mistake, but the house was locked up and silent. He walked around the back and stood in the yard, feeling completely lost. God had led him to his daughter and now she was gone. It was almost more than he could bear. Then came the Savior's comforting voice.

Heed my word and you will see her again.

"Thy will be done, Lord," he declared.

With the Lord's will firmly instilled in his mind, Greg acquired the truck, then spent a good part of the morning loading The St. John's storage. When he finished, he headed home to pack a bag, making a stop along the way to purchase a tent and camping equipment, as well as some other things he was prompted to buy. He did not question anything, he just obeyed.

Early the next morning as he was leaving his apartment for good, the McDonald family pulled up in their minivan and said they were counseled to follow him.

And now here they are.

Greg tells the two armed men at the gate who he is and they open it and let him and the family in, promptly locking it behind them. He parks the truck in a dirt area and grabs his backpack, sleeping bag, tent, and another large duffle bag. He would need to bring back help for the food. The McDonalds grab their things and follow Greg through the dry, high grassy field and into the trees.

The camp is quite a ways and Greg has to slow his step a little. He is anxious to get there, but he can't get too far ahead of the McDonalds, so he forces himself to steady his pace, which is no easy thing.

Because he knows what awaits him at the camp. His family.

As I promised myself I would, I get up with Adagio and ready myself for the day. The leftover biscuit from last night's dinner helps to keep the nausea at bay until breakfast.

While Adagio is out helping where he is needed, I tidy up the tent. When he gets back, he compliments me on my housekeeping skills, making me laugh. I tell him it isn't very hard.

I need to establish a routine, and I decide that from now on while Adagio is out helping around the camp, I will do school with Dagio. He is reading well and his spelling is excellent. When Adagio comes back, he will go over the math with him. Then we will read scriptures together. Adagio says it sounds like a great routine.

A while later, new people enter the camp from the opposite direction we came. As they get closer, I can see that it is a family. They are following an attractive older gentleman. The man carries himself like an experienced leader. Everyone in the group is loaded down with a backpack and camping gear.

As Eban heads out to greet them, Dagio shoots past us yelling, "Grandpa Greg!" and I gasp.

"Greg!" My voice is a whisper. Adagio puts an arm around me.

"Yes," he affirms, joy filling his voice. "That is Greg, angel."

I watch Greg drop everything and catch Dagio in his arms, lifting him and hugging him close. Dagio wraps his arms around his neck.

After a moment, Greg puts Dagio down, shakes hand with Eban (they seem to know each other already) and introduces the family. Eban then calls the men to come and help unload the truck Greg drove up.

"Come," Adagio says, taking my hand.

When Greg looks our way, tears fill his eyes and he smiles.

Adagio hugs him. "We're so glad to see you."

"I'm glad to see you too."

Adagio leaves to go help the men. Greg turns to me and gently says my name. He opens his arms, reaching for my hand and I move into his embrace, crying as I hold onto him.

"I didn't think we would see you again," I say against his shoulder.

"I know. I was afraid of that too. But I was wrong to doubt." He releases an emotional chuckle. "And now you know what I have been doing since I moved here."

I draw back and touch his wet face. "You look just like Adagio described." I smile at his widening hazel eyes.

"Do you mean . . ."

"Yes. I can see."

"But . . . how?"

"I was healed on Christmas night."

"That's amazing!" He hugs me again. "It's a miracle!"

"I am sure there will be many more. In fact . . . I already have a second miracle growing inside me."

Greg sucks in a breath. "Really? You're going to have a baby?"

"I am."

"Well, that explains it," he murmurs.

"Explains what?"

He smiles, pressing a hand to my cheek and squeezing the other. "I will tell you later. In fact, I need to tell you something else as well."

"Okay." I squeeze his hand. "I'm so glad you're here."

"Me, too, Evangeline. Me, too."

Chapter 13

Sometimes Heavenly Father will answer a prayer before a word is even uttered. He does not need to hear our prayers to know our heart, but we need to pray to know His.

Adagio St. John's Journal

*O*nce everything is brought to the camp site, we visit with Greg while he sets up his tent in an area near ours. He had purchased the same model so it doesn't take long. Afterward, he brings our little propane heater to us and hands me the duffle bag he'd carried into camp.

"When I was prompted to purchase these things,

I didn't question it, I simply obeyed. But first . . . Adagio, I need to borrow your wife for a bit." He smiles, his eyes tinged with a sadness I can't help wondering about.

"Of course," Adagio says. "I'll just put this in the tent for Evangeline." He kisses me. "Enjoy your visit."

Adagio

As Adagio watches Greg and Evangeline walk away hand in hand, he smiles, swallowing against the emotion rising inside him and blinks the tears away. He has been holding the truth about Greg inside since the moment the Savior revealed it to him. As much as Adagio had wanted to share it with his wife, it had not been his news to share, and he wouldn't have taken that opportunity away even if he could. When he'd learned who Greg really is, his heart had practically burst with joy for Evangeline. He had considered it a miracle. Then he'd gone into the house and discovered she could see. It had been an entire night of miracles!

Taking the duffle bag inside the tent, he opens it, his smile growing wider as he fingers the baby things. There are also clothes for Evangeline for both cold and warm weather that will stretch to accommodate her growing stomach during the pregnancy. Greg had definitely been inspired, and Adagio offers up a prayer of thanks in his and Evangeline's behalf.

Closing his eyes, Adagio utters another quick prayer that all will be well with Greg and Evangeline. They need each other more now than ever.

"She will be fine, son."

He turns at the sound of the soft masculine voice, a voice that is one of the most beloved he knows.

"NONNUCCIO. NONNINA." HIS VOICE IS FILLED WITH AWE AT THE SIGHT OF HIS GRANDPARENTS BEFORE HIM. "IT IS SO GOOD TO SEE YOU."

"It is good to see you too," he grandmother says. "But truthfully, we are never far away."

"I have felt you near many times. Usually when I have been troubled."

"You have been strong," his grandfather says. "And your faith is sure. It will prepare you for what will soon come. The days of tribulation are upon this world and you and your little family will endure much. All the faithful will."

"Carrying a child through this will not be easy for Evangeline," his grandmother tells him. "She will need your strength."

"I will give her all that I have. With God's help, I will take care of my wife and son."

"We know you will," his grandfather says.

"Do you know how Mama and Papa are? And Evangeline's mother, and my sisters?"

"They are well," his grandfather assures him. "They have gathered and found refuge. Your uncles and aunt and their families have as well."

Adagio heaves a small sigh of relief. He'd had faith that his family was okay, but hearing it from his grandparents is comforting.

"We love you, Adagio," his grandmother says, her eyes full of love.

"And remember, we are always near," his grandfather reminds him.

"I love you both. And thank you."

We stop and sit on a fallen log. For a moment Greg says nothing. I watch the puffs of fog escape through his lips, his nose red from the cold. I take in his handsome mature features. His hazel eyes finally meet mine and his expression almost looks fearful.

"Greg," I say, squeezing his hand, "you can tell me anything."

His opens his mouth to speak but doesn't say anything. Instead, he pulls a red and green striped envelope from inside his coat and places it in my hand. There is a candy cane and a sprig of Christmas holly attached to the front

"This is the Christmas gift I was going to give you before you left. When you open it, I hope you will understand that I didn't . . . when I realized, I . . ." He stops, swallowing hard and pressing his lips together, the lines etched around his eyes becoming deeper.

Taking the candy cane and holly off and stuffing them in my coat pocket, I open the envelope and remove the paper, unfolding it.

It is a birth certificate–a generic computer-generated one, but it is still a certificate of birth. It has my name printed on the top line, as well as my place of birth, Atlanta, Georgia. The birth statistic blanks are empty. My eyes slowly travel to the birth mother, then to the birth father, my blurring vision settling on Greg's name.

For a moment I can only stare. Then my mind is

opened and things slowly begin to fall into place. Amazingly, I can see everything.

I see Greg's humble childhood, the loss of his mother, and I see his life while living on the streets. I can feel his burning desire to make a better life for himself.

I see Greg meeting my mother.

Her drug abuse and betrayal.

My birth and her death.

His choice to let me go and the consequences of that choice.

The pain of regret he felt.

The love he found with his wife and the joy that came with discovering the gospel.

The sorrow of losing his wife to cancer.

And finally, the never ending desire that burned within him to find me and make amends.

I finally lift my eyes to his, reading the fear and sadness in them. "When did you find out?"

"I realized you . . . that you were my daughter the day you were out visiting. I was eating the cake you made and talking with Adagio. He was telling me about your life and . . . things began to click. When the full truth of it dawned on me, it took everything to hold myself together. I felt so much joy to finally have my daughter in my life, to know how you turned out, but I was also more afraid than I had ever been in my life. In all these years, not a day has gone by that I didn't wish I could take back what I did. The decision to turn my back on you was the worst I have ever made."

With tears in his eyes, Greg kneels in front of me. "I am so sorry, Evangeline. I'm so sorry. I wish I could make up for what I did. I wish I could take it back, but I can't. Can you ever forgive me for abandoning you? Can you give me the chance to be your father, to try to be the father you deserve? I know I will never be worthy of you, but I will spend the rest of eternity trying."

I press a hand against his wet cheek as tears spill down mine. "I forgive you, Dad," I say simply. "I forgave you a long time ago, and I am grateful for the opportunity to tell you. I love you, and I'm grateful to know you and have you in my life now."

He hugs me, breathing a small sob and I wrap my arms around his neck, holding him close.

My father. Greg is my father. My Heavenly Father

has blessed me with my earthly one. Joy fills my heart, so much that it bubbles to the surface and I laugh.

Drawing back, I touch his face again. "If I could have chosen a man to be my father here on earth, it would have been you. From the moment we met you, I have felt an unexplainable connection to you. Now I know why."

"I felt the same."

I smile, touching his slightly-graying waves. "I look forward to meeting my mother one day, but until then, I look forward to you being able to know the mother that raised me."

"I look forward to meeting her as well. I know about your tough relationship with her growing up, but I understand from your husband that a great change came over her, and I would like to thank her for giving you the privileged life that I couldn't."

"I would gladly give the privilege that came with that life back just to have this time with you."

His tears renew and we stand, and I just hold him, more grateful than I can say for this most unexpected gift.

When we get back to camp, Adagio is waiting, and in his eyes I see pure joy. Holding me close, he whispers, "I have known since the night we left, but I could not say anything. It was not my news to tell."

"I know."

Closing my eyes, I soak in the warmth of his embrace, grateful to know that despite the hard times ahead, miracles will still abound. God will mingle the bitter with the sweet, and somehow we will make it through as long as we are obedient.

Later in the day, a woman arrives alone. On her back is a small backpack, a two-person tent, and a sleeping bag. She pulls a large suitcase behind her. I go with Adagio and Dad to welcome her. Her name is Gwen, and she tells us her husband and teenage son abandoned her and left for Las Vegas. Her husband has always had a gambling problem and is now passing it on to their son.

Gwen's son had been a budding musician and had left some instruments behind that she was prompted to bring with her. She opens her suitcase, and to mine and Adagio's surprise, among her few things is a violin wrapped in a cloth and a small portable keyboard. She even has extra batteries.

"Maybe someone can use these," she says.

Dad chuckles, looking at us. "Oh, I think we can find someone who can."

Two months later, an invitation is extended to the saints to gather to various places of refuge and a mere three-hundred souls join our camp.

Sadly, many choose not to listen, deciding to wait until things get worse.

They will not have to wait long.

For nation shall rise against nation, and kingdom against kingdom: and there shall be famines, and pestilences, and earthquakes, in divers places. All these are the beginning of sorrows.

Matthew 24: 7-8

Chapter 14

A man truly is half a man without a helpmeet. God in his infinite wisdom sent me the choicest. For me, speaking the phrase, "My wife," is equivalent to saying, "I am."

Adagio St. John's Journal

Adagio

Like in other places of refuge, the saints in the little city spend their days in spiritual preparation, praying for the people of the country, and for themselves.

Like Adagio's family, everyone has developed a routine to help pass the days. Each family sees to their own personal needs, trying to form some semblance of a normal life, though things are far from normal. The camp shares main meals together, each person taking a turn to do their part in the cleanup and upkeep. On Sundays, they meet in the large common area where they have sacrament meeting and listen to messages by Eban and others invited by him to speak to the congregation. Adagio and Evangeline joyfully provide music for the hymns on the keyboard and violin, bringing a special spirit to the meeting.

Partaking of the sacrament is an especially holy experience and is what the members need to keep them going week after week.

Before being called to this preparation assignment, Eban had been a bishop, and though he was released, he was called to be a leader over the camp. Just before the official invitation to gather, he was again called and set apart as a bishop. After praying about the two men who should be his counselors, a call was extended to Adagio and Greg. Both men happily accepted. Because Adagio was already serving a great deal of the time, he isn't any busier now, but he is happy his responsibilities are official and does his best to let the spirit guide him in everything.

Adagio grows more and more in love with his wife with each passing day, and there is nothing that he would not do for her. She tries so hard to do her part and not be a burden–which she could never be–and she never complains when morning sickness keeps her confined to the tent. She bears it with grace and tries to be positive in every word and action. She is being so brave and strong. She doesn't think she's strong, but she is, and she is an example to him and everyone else in their refuge city. Of the seven women in their group carrying a child, she is the oldest, but looking at her, you cannot tell. She doesn't look a day over twenty-five, and on the days that she is well enough to leave the tent, she is always active, trying to be of help in any capacity she can.

Today is an uncharacteristically warm day for the mountains. Adagio has spent a good part of the morning studying nature with Dagio for school. He always enjoys these one-on-one times with his son and treasures the close relationship they share. Though he knows Dagio and Evangeline are especially close, Adagio is coming to share something just as special with him. Maybe it is because the cares of daily life they once had are no more, the gain of material possessions and pursuits are irrelevant, and all thoughts are now fixed on the important things. In any case, there is joy in each new day, even more so than before, and Adagio is grateful for this time of growth.

After Dagio runs off to see Brad and Alicia, Adagio enters the tent to check on his wife. Evangeline had had an especially bad morning, but after taking in a little soup and drinking some ginger tea, her stomach calmed and she was able to sleep a little. He stretches out next to her, caressing her cheek.

"How are you feeling, *dolcezza*?"

"Better," she sighs. "Thanks for taking care of Dagio."

"You don't need to thank me, angel. Taking care of you and Dagio is my place."

She gives him a teary smile. "Hopefully I will get past this soon and won't be a –"

"You are not a burden," he breaks in gently.

"You will never be. Please do not think that." Leaning in, he kisses her lips and looks into her eyes. "Do not ever think that again. Promise me."

"I promise."

He presses a hand back over her hair, fingering the soft curls. "When was the last time I told you how beautiful you are?"

She snorts, making him laugh. "You tell me the moment I wake in the mornings, though I have to question your eyesight when my hair is a complete mess and there are permanent circles beneath my eyes these days."

"Your hair is never a mess, just attractively wild, and I do not see circles, I only see your beautiful brown eyes gazing at me. I cannot see anything else." He kisses her, reveling in the feel of her hand on his face, in his hair. Drawing her close to his side, he wraps her in his arms.

"*Ti amo, bella,*" he murmurs against her mouth.

"*Ti amo, vita mia.*" She rests her head against his chest.

Adagio tightens his embrace and sighs. He lay listening to her breathing deepen and she is soon sleeping again. After a few minutes, he drifts to sleep with his lips against her brow.

A short while later, they are awakened by a loud rumbling and shaking of the ground. They quickly sit up, looking at each other as they realize what is happening.

Dagio rushes into the tent. "Mama," he says, moving into her open arms.

Adagio looks out the tent window. Everyone is gathering their families and moving to their tents.

Wrapping his arms around his wife and son, Adagio's prayers join theirs.

Then his heart immediately calms, and peace stills his soul.

Chapter 15

God's word is always sure, and His warnings have been a tender mercy, a gift that many refused. That hour of acceptance has long passed.

Adagio St. John's Journal

$\mathcal{L}$ast month an earthquake registering 6.5 on the Richter scale hit Salt Lake City, doing some serious damage to downtown, and North and South Salt Lake.

Two days later, an earthquake registering 9.2 in magnitude hit the west coast destroying most of California, Oregon and Washington. The casualties reached tens of thousands. People who had heeded the earlier calling and promptings to flee to prepared places of refuge were kept safe. Some managed to make it to smaller tent cities. Members of other religions also fled to the camps and were welcomed. The rest suffered dearly.

Yes, it was a deadly-tragic earthquake and the damage caused to the west coast was catastrophic.

But the second earthquake that hit Salt Lake City stretching along the Wasatch Front just two days ago was just as deadly and has completely demolished the city. By the time the report came in, thousands of lives were lost, thousands of homes were lost, and the main roads in and out of the city were blocked by debris. A large chunk of I-15 at the point of the mountain is no longer there. In its place now is a massive sinkhole lake that fills the mile-wide drop-off.

Another large earthquake hits Nevada and southern Utah a week later. Though the damage isn't the size and scope of the second Salt Lake earthquake, it is still bad and there are lives lost.

Soon after, looting and rioting escalate, making the valley a dangerous place to be.

Then comes a deadly man-made plague, one that has never been seen before. The contagion is high and there is no cure. Hundreds die daily.

The foreign troops that began invading our soil long ago–right under the noses of the majority of American citizens–unleash their havoc on the country by seeking out and rounding up surviving Americans, herding them into concentration camps, and perpetrating all manner of evil before exterminating them.

Then another disease begins to spread through the troops and many die despite being inoculated.

Soon after, another earthquake measuring 8.5 in magnitude hits the Great Lakes, practically splitting the country in two.

It is through the miraculous workings of the Church's transmission system– undetected internet and radio channels–that we stay informed. The First Presidency and the Quorum of the Twelve still run the church and do what they can to keep track of God's people. Our city of refuge, as well as the other refuge cities have been surrounded in heavenly protection, kept safe from disease and the troops. Unfortunately, we have had a few brushes with groups of stragglers stumbling upon our camp and most of them are not friendly. The few who are, we are inspired to help with food and clothing, and though they are invited to stay, they choose to move on. As for the others, after harsh words and a few gunshots fired by the men guarding the gate, the groups move on. Every man, including my husband and my father, keeps a firearm nearby, ready to load if needed.

However, we soon find it is unnecessary because we have become completely shielded by heavenly protection, so much so that our camp is literally undetectable.

We are told that most of the countries are in chaos because of natural disasters and the cold hearts of men, but those who have gathered are safe and being watched over. In our hearts, Adagio and I know our family is all right, and we look forward to the day when we can see them again.

And that reunion will happen in New Jerusalem.

On August 15th, after the longest six hours of my

life, Adagio delivers our healthy daughter. We name her after Adagio's beloved grandmother. Letting out a boisterous cry, flailing her long arms and legs, she is beautiful, and we don't need a scale to know that she is at least eight pounds.

When the labor first started, it hit hard and fast. Dad kept Dagio with him and once Adagio got everything we would need in order, he never left my side. There are a couple of doctor in our camp, but one was so ill, he was bedridden. The other was handling a virus outbreak that had trickled into camp. But I didn't worry. Adagio had delivered Dagio at home and was very capable. He had been patient, loving, and strong, and with Heavenly Father's help, all had gone smoothly.

Now I lay weakened from the loss of too much blood. Holding little Cisely close to my side, my blurry eyes take in the tears trailing down my husband's face, my ears listening to his repeated murmur of "*Sei l'amore della mia vita.* You are the love of my life. I won't lose you. It is not your time."

Looking into Adagio's eyes, an entry he read me from his grandfather's journal comes to mind. Adagio's grandmother had been in a car accident and his grandfather had been in anguish, worried that he would lose her, but trying to have faith that he wouldn't.

I sat by Cisely's bedside all night, and the soft light of the morning casted an illuminating glow on her face. I did not sleep at all and had spent the entire night gazing at her face and holding her hand. Her cheek was bruised and swollen, but I still never saw a more beautiful face. After talking with Peter earlier and hearing the extent of her injuries, it was a miracle she was still alive.

Peter told me Cisely had two cracked ribs, a broken leg, a broken wrist, and a severe concussion. He said that because she had not regained consciousness, it was possible for her to slip into a coma. He also said there was a chance she may never wake up. That was something I could not think about. I just couldn't.

I moved to the head of the bed, rested my head next to hers on the pillow, and talked to her. I told her how much I loved her.

"Please come back to me. I need you more than

you could ever know, more than words could ever express. I could not bear it if I lost you. You are my whole life, and if I lost you, I would die, too. I know I would."

I pressed a hand to her face, caressing it softly, needing to touch her. "I need you to come back to me, amore. Our children need you. They need their mother. I need my wife. I need the love you give to me, the joy you bring to my life every day."

I tenderly traced the outline of her lips with my finger and softly touched the bandaged spot on her temple. As I did, my thoughts traveled to a couple of nights ago and the intimacy we shared. It had been indescribable and unlike anything I have ever experienced. Intimacy between us has always been amazing, but that night it had been something else entirely. I had held her afterward and drifted to sleep with tears clogging my throat. I love her so much.

"We still have so many years left, angel," I continued to tell her. "So many years to live and love on this earth. We need to grow old together, to watch each other's hair turn white and watch our children raise their children. I can't do any of those things *without you. I have to have you here with me. I know you will always be mine even in death, but I need you here with me now. You are my everything, baby." I pressed a gentle kiss to her lips, grateful they were still warm.*

I did not want to leave her, but I finally went home to shower and check on our family. When I returned to my beloved's side, I fell asleep with my head on the bed next to her side. Then I was awakened by her gentle touch and joy filled my heart. It had not been her time to leave me after all. We still had years ahead of us. For the rest of my days, I will thank God for that.

I remember how we both cried as Adagio read, imagining what his grandfather must have been going through, how scared he must have been. Adagio told me how he prayed frequently that he would never be faced with the possibility of losing me, because he would literally die too.

"It is not your time, *amore*," Adagio repeats, drawing me back to the present, his voice soft but firm.

Placing his hands on my head with Dad

assisting, and according to the God's will, Adagio uses his priesthood power and blesses me, commanding my body to be made whole. The healing is instant, the bleeding stops and my strength is returned tenfold. In fact, I don't even feel like a woman who has just given birth. I sit up and Adagio gathers me to him, kissing my brow over and over. I smile up at him, then look at my father and smile. He wipes the tears from his face.

"Would you like to hold your granddaughter?" I ask.

"I would love to."

I hand her to him and he cradles her in the crook of his arm.

"She's beautiful like her mama. And I guess I can see a little of her papa." He grins at Adagio and Adagio laughs.

Dad leaves us alone with our daughter, sending Dagio in a few minutes later. He crawls over and joins us and I place his sister in his arms.

We quietly enjoy this serene time together in our cozy tent and I am again grateful to call it home. It will mostly likely be our home for a long while yet.

Sixteen

Sacrifice is a giant of a word, a word that took on new meaning the moment we left all our possessions. A word that is about to expose another layer our true selves–expose what we are made of.

Adagio St. John's Journal

One Year Later

Adagio

This morning the camp got word from the prophet. They are to leave tomorrow and will begin their trek across the United States to Jackson County, Missouri where they will help to build New Jerusalem in preparation for the Savior's return. Adagio and his family have been looking forward to this day from the moment they entered the camp almost two years ago, and now the time is finally here.

After packing up most of their things and placing them in our small handcart (Eban received the construction plans a month ago and had each family build one) Adagio's family turn in early because they will be starting out at sunrise. Dagio is so excited, it takes a while for him to fall asleep, but he eventually does. Little Cisely is asleep next to Evangeline. The year-old toddler is worn out from playing with her brother and his friends.

Adagio holds his wife close as they discuss the past year and speculate over the upcoming trek.

Over the past year, the United States was virtually destroyed as God's wrath was poured out upon it. Man warred against the elements and lost. And not just this country. The whole earth was in commotion.

All businesses were closed and the righteous of the country were still in hiding, kept safe by the Lord.

For months, men age eighteen and over traveled

from each camp and banded together in New Mexico to defend the country and take it back from the remaining troops. They all went to war armed, there was fighting, and many lives were lost, including a few men from Adagio's own celestial city, for that is indeed what the Lord now calls his camp.

Every day that Adagio and Greg were away, they prayed for Evangeline and the children, as well as the rest of the camp, invoking the Lord's blessings upon them. Adagio prayed that he would make it back to his family, but he had been willing to die in defense of the constitution, even though Washington D.C. abandoned it long ago, setting the country up to fall. And fall it has.

With the defeat of the foreign troops came the paving of the way for the people to start the long journey across the land to their new home.

When Adagio and the other men returned, he and Evangeline cried tears of joy as they held one another. After hugging her father and welcoming him back as well, she told Adagio about another comforting visit from his grandparents. They had assured her all was well with the family and encouraged her to be strong. They told her it would not be long before they were all together again. Adagio wished he had been there, but he is grateful Evangeline had been comforted.

Pulling his thoughts to the present, Adagio draws his wife closer, sighing as her arm tightens around his waist. The hot August day has cooled, the night temperature perfect for snuggling.

"It is an ideal time to leave," Adagio murmurs against her brow. "But I know it will get rough in a couple of months once the weather turns colder."

"It will be a trial for all," she says. "But it will be worth it." She sighs. "Since food supplies are so low, there will not be enough to even see us through the trek, much less when we finally do get there. But I guess that is where the miracles will come in."

Adagio makes a soft noise in agreement. Each family had been given part of what was left of the food. The lack of a sufficient amount had weighed on his mind for a short while. The thought of his wife and children suffering as the early saints did as they trekked from Nauvoo to Salt Lake City hurt his heart, but the Lord had comforted him, and now Adagio knows with absolute certainty that God will show forth His power. And Adagio received a confirmation that his little family will make it because he and Evangeline will be needed for their strength. As long as they lose themselves in love and be the Lord's hands on the trek, their children will be taken care of. Evangeline had received this confirmation as well.

Adagio kisses Evangeline and they say goodnight.

"*Ti amo,*" she whispers.

"*Ti amo,*" he whispers back, drawing her further into himself, pressing his lips to her ear. "*Ti amo con tutta me stessa.* I love you with all my heart." She snuggles against him and sighs.

Adagio's final thought as he drifts to sleep is of the Savior's words to him earlier in the day.

You and Evangeline were foreordained for this task. Many will depend on you. Be my hands.

It is a little after dawn when the saints gather for a prayer. Their hearts are filled with gratitude to be leaving for Missouri, and they kneel in humble supplication for Heavenly Father's protection on their journey.

Then grabbing their handcarts, they line up and head out.

Seventeen

And so it begins.

Like the pioneers before us, we go forward with faith in every footstep.

Adagio St. John's Journal

For the first month, we travel twenty miles a day. We set up camp each night and start out again at sunrise, resting periodically throughout the day. The youth and small children keep spirits up and aid in passing the days in joy. During this time, many of the youth begin to dream dreams and see visions of things to come pertaining to the coming of the Savior. In their innocence, their minds are being opened and they are being prepared. It brings comfort to us all.

Then, due growing fatigue, illness comes to many of the older members of our group and we begin to cover less ground.

A bout of the flu sweeps through the camp and many become sick, mainly the children and the older adults. The priesthood is utilized and Eban, Adagio, Dad and some of the other healthy priesthood holders administer blessings to the sick. With so many falling ill, we are forced to stop and set up camp for almost a week.

In our tent, I care for Dagio and Cisely as best I can, holding and rocking them, making them as comfortable as possible.

On the third day of sickness during a moment that Dagio is awake, he asks me, "Will I die, Mama? Will Cisely die?"

"No, baby," I assure him. "You and your sister will be well. We were promised by the Lord that our family will make it to New Jerusalem."

"Will others die?"

As much as I wish I could say no, I know I must

be honest with him. "Yes," I finally answer, caressing his moist brow. "But God is watching over us all, and those that die will be safe in His arms. They will be all right."

"Okay," he says, seeming satisfied with my answer. I give him a chewable vitamin C pill and some liquid Echinacea and put a cool cloth on his forehead.

"Let your mind be at ease, son," Adagio says. "No matter what we have to face, the Lord will be with us."

"That's what He told me, Papa."

Adagio smiles then gives Dagio a blessing of comfort.

Cisely soon awakens and cries for me. I change her diaper and damp t-shirt. Giving her a few sips of water mixed with vitamin C powder, I massage her arms, legs, feet, and stomach with some essential oils, and I hold her close, rocking her until she falls asleep again. I softly brush the dark curls back from her face. Her hair is unusually long and thick for a one-year-old and reaches just past her shoulders. While Dagio looks just like his father, Cisely's features are a mixture of both of ours, but her light brown eyes are definitely mine.

I lay her down next to her brother who is sleeping again and go with Adagio to check on others, offering what comfort I can. Dad joins us.

For some, the flu advances into pneumonia. Most are able to pull through, but a few succumb and graves are dug. Though there is sadness with each passing, there is also peace in knowing they no longer suffer and are in a better place. Some, I am sure, stick close by to watch over loved ones they've left behind.

Three weeks away from our destination, the temperature cools significantly, and with the coming of snow comes the slow descent of hunger as the food runs out.

As for Adagio and me, and Dad as well, we seem to grow stronger and somehow are able to survive on less than the others. The cold hasn't affected us as much as it should, either. It is as if our bodies are somehow changing. We still drink water whenever we can find it, but we don't feel starved, so most of our food has been going to our children, as well as our extra blankets. Dad gives away his extra blankets as well, wanting to help others out.

Adagio and I sleep each night wrapped in each other's arms, comforted that our children are warm enough. Many in the group don't have that luxury, and we pray for them constantly.

One night I quietly ask Adagio, "Why do you think our bodies are changing and not the others?"

"I don't know, *amore*. I wonder as well. But God has His reasons. I am sure He will make it known in time." He is quiet for a moment and I know he is thinking. "Maybe it has been a refining process and somehow we have been found worthy. Not that the others are not. Or maybe He found us ready because we were watching and waiting. Whatever the reason, I am grateful to be used in the Lord's service."

"So am I."

We receive another visit from Adagio's grandparents. They speak of their love for us and offer encouragement and comfort. They also assure us that our family is well. They have visited with Adagio's parents and informed them of our well-being. No other details are shared, which is fine with us. We would like to know more, but we are comforted to know everyone is well and look forward to being with them again when it is time.

I have come to love Adagio and Cisely St. John so much, and I always miss them after they are gone, but I know we will see them again.

Soon the food completely runs out and the camp is immersed in hunger.

Then the miracles begin.

We wake up one morning to find cakes of manna on the ground. After humble prayers of gratitude, each family stores enough for several days. The food from heaven tastes like heaven.

This miracle happens two more times, sustaining the strength of the group a while longer. It does not happen again until we finally reach what will be New Jerusalem.

As our exhausted group crosses into the abandoned city, surrounded by destruction and abandoned homes and buildings in every direction, we drop to our knees and cry tears of joy.

"We made it," I say, emotion clogging my throat. Adagio squeezes my hand, echoing my sentiments.

We know the task before us. We know it will not be easy, but God has led us to our new home, to build it up for His Son's return. More groups will arrive soon, and we know we won't have to do it alone.

None of us will ever be alone again.

J. Adams

Epilogue

Many, Many Years Later

Adagio

$\mathcal{S}$ince the time of Christ's crucifixion, the faithful had looked to his second coming. Throughout each generation, for many, the longing for His return never waned, but grew stronger with the passing of time. As much as man tried to imagine that day, no words even came close to describing the awaited event that took place so many years ago. That day had come and is now part of the history of this world. And Adagio and his family had witnessed it all.

The sound of the joyful voices of his family

draws Adagio's thoughts to the present and he lets his eyes travel over his many loved ones, feeling that exquisite joy deep inside him. At the squeeze of Evangeline's hand, he turns to her and smiles, bringing it to his lips. They are sitting on the veranda of their Italian villa. In no way does it resemble his old family home, but it is home to them. They are surrounded in celestial splendor that defies description. Everything is more vivid–the colors, the sounds, the fresh earthy smell.

On either side of Adagio and Evangeline sit his parents and grandparents. Out on the lawn visiting are Evangeline's mother, Katherine, her father, Greg, and his wife, Page.

Althea, Evangeline's biological mother, is also present. She is sitting on a bench visiting with Jessica, the woman Adagio's grandparents inherited the house in Salt Lake from, and her nephew, Ingo, who was once married to Adagio's grandmother. Ingo and Althea are holding hands, having found happiness in each other. Jessica is also married, having found love after being alone during her mortal life. Adagio watches her turn to her husband as he approaches them and it warms his heart.

Adagio's siblings, uncles, aunt, cousins, and other relatives, including many of his ancestors, are here as well.

But moving before them all is the Savior.

As He approaches, Adagio and Evangeline stand, taking His offered hands, basking in the radiance of His smile.

"The Father needs you," the Savior tells them. "There is some final work to be done."

"Yes, Master," Adagio says reverently.

The Savior smiles and turns to leave, stopping to visit with the family along the way. Adagio again smiles at his wife.

No, his imagination could never have done these days justice.

Words will never be good enough.

About The Author

J. (Jewel) Adams stays crazy busy with her family and writing. She has written several books in different genres and is also a motivational speaker to both youth and adult audiences.

In her spare time (when she has any) she likes to curl up with a good book and a healthy stash of orange Tic Tacs. She and her family reside in Utah.

Jewel loves hearing from her fans. You can contact her at jewela40@gmail.com

Visit Jewels Blog at jewelsbestgems.blogspot.com